SEALSKIN
TROUSERS

General Editor: Gerald Konyn

SEALSKIN
TROUSERS

AND OTHER STORIES

ERIC LINKLATER

With wood engravings by
Joan Hassall

LARGE PRINT
MASTERWORKS

First published in 1947
by Rupert Hart-Davis,
London

Published in Large Print 1989
by arrangement with A.D. Peters &
Company Limited

A joint imprint of ISIS Large Print Books,
55 St. Thomas' Street, Oxford OX1 1JG
and Guild Large Print Books Ltd
25 High Street, Lewes, Sussex

Photosetting in Times 20 pt by
Futura Typesetters, Hove, Sussex
and printed in Great Britain by
Antony Rowe Ltd, Chippenham, Wiltshire

ISBN 1 85290 021 0

Jacket design by Douglas Quiggan
and Robert Soudain. Title page
design by Robert Soudain. Portrait of
Eric Linklater by Bob Bowdige

CONTENTS

THE GOOSE GIRL

THE GOOSE GIRL

When I woke among the currant-bushes I saw her coming out of the cottage door with her fist round the gander's neck. I heard them too, for she was yelling and the gander was beating the doorposts and beating her thighs with his great creaking wings. Like a windmill in the distance, like the slap of a rising swan's black feet on the water, like clothes on the line thrashing in a breeze: the gander was making nearly as much noise as she

9

was, and she was shouting her head off. There was no leaping tune in her voice that morning. It was just the air in her lungs being driven through the funnel of her throat like steam from a well-fired boiler; and some of the words she was using were no prettier than what goes on in any stoker's mind. But I wasn't listening so much as looking. I had heard those words before, but I had never seen a woman's body like hers, so firm and long of limb, like a young reed in firmness and round as an apple where it should be, and white as a pearl. Against the gander's wings, which were a cold white like snow, her pallor was warm and glowing. Not reflecting light, but glowing with it. She was naked as the sky, and the sky, at four o'clock in the morning, was bare of cloud except for a little twist of wool low down in the west.

Now she gripped the gander's neck with both her hands, and even her hands weren't red like any other country girl's, but small and white. They were strong though, and I could see the hardness of her forearms. She was throttling the bird, and its beak was wide open, a gaping stretch of yellow skin, the upper mandible at right-angles to the lower. Its eyes were hidden in the ruffling of its little head-feathers. She dragged it through the door, gave a great heave, and threw it with a noise of breaking stalks into some overgrown rhubarb. A splash of dew-drops rose from the leaves and caught the light. For a moment she stood looking at the bird, her arms a little bent and her hair dishevelled, her mouth open, and her breast rising and falling. Then, abruptly, she turned and went back into the

11

cottage, slamming the door behind her. I listened, I remember, for the sound of a key turning or a bolt going home; but in this part of the country they never lock their doors. It was lack of custom, not lack of feeling, that prevented her from giving this final emphasis to her act of expulsion.

The gander shook himself, hissing loudly, and broke more stalks of rhubarb as he made his way to a narrow path of little sea-shore pebbles. I had seen him before, half a dozen times with the girl, and always marvelled at the size of him, but now, from where I lay among the currant-bushes, he looked bigger than ever and his ruffled head-feathers stood out like a crown. His neck was as stiff as a broom-handle but twice as thick, and he turned his head this way and that with a twitch of the bill, an angry snap. His little black eyes were swollen and bright, and the broad webs of his feet fell on the path with the heavy tread of German infantry. He stopped when he saw me and stood for a little while, hissing like a burst tyre; but not in the way of an ordinary gander, with its neck low to the ground and its beak reaching forward.

He stood upright, his head swaying back as if to look at me from a greater height, and when he had done with hissing he turned his back on me and went tramping through some rows of cabbage-plants to a gap in the low garden wall where the old turf-dyke on which it was built had collapsed and brought down the stone. It was a plain little garden with no colour in it except some yellow daisies under the cottage windows and a thin growth of honeysuckle

13

beside the door. There was a fuchsia hedge on one side, not in flower yet, and gooseberries and black-currant bushes along the other walls, with a clump of grey-barked elder-trees in the corner. On one side of the dividing pebble-path rhubarb and spring onions, early potatoes and cabbage on the other: that was all. And the gander, marching like a Prussian, flattened the cabbages under his broad splayed feet as if there had been the weight of a man in him. Perhaps there was. He was no ordinary bird, that was certain.

I got up and followed him, cautiously, as he disappeared, and watched him swimming down the little stream that runs behind the cottage to the big loch a quarter of a mile away. I saw his head, still ruffled, still indignantly twitching, behind a bank of meadowsweet; and then he vanished.

I leant against the wall of a cartshed, thinking. The air was still, and the country looked as though no one had ever touched it. The day before had been wet and ugly, and I remembered with a kind of shame how unhappy I had been; and how clumsily I had behaved, getting drunk so that I could tell the truth. But now I felt uncommonly well – and I had done my duty. There's nothing like sleeping in the open air to prevent a hangover, and I had, after long delay, disburdened my mind. The evening before I had gone to see John Norquoy to tell him how his young brother had been killed on the shore of Lake Commachio.

We had been together for a long time, Jim Norquoy and I, in the Seaforths to begin with and then in the Commando, and between Primo Sole in Sicily and that great cold lagoon of Commachio, mud and water and a dancing mirage, we had had our fill of fighting. Jim was hit in shallow water, wading ashore after our boats had grounded on a mudbank just as the sun came up, and I carried him in. But he died on the edge of the land, and his last words were, 'You'll find it difficult to go back too, after all this.'

That was an understatement. I found it impossible to go back to the life I had known before, and when I came north to the islands, to tell his people about Jim and give him what immortality I could, be feeding their pride in him, I was looking for something for myself as well. No more school-teaching for me. I was never meant to be a teacher anyway, either by Providence or my parents.

I had only wanted to live – I mean to live in such a way that life came in through my eyes and I could feel it on my skin – but never had I known how to go about it till the war came. And now, when the war was over, I was more at a loss than ever. I couldn't go back to an elementary school in Falkirk, and teach little boys the parts of speech and the more blatant pieces of history, for fear that one of them, some day, might ask me, 'What's it all for? What are we going to say when we've learnt the parts of speech; and if we learn all the history in the world, what would it mean?'

I was no coward, not in the physical sense, and I had been a good soldier – not as good as Jim, though I earned my pay – but when I looked at those questions in the solitude of my mind I knew that I couldn't face them in public. Nor did I want to. I wanted to live, but not to set myself up as a preceptor of living. As a small boy I had gone about in a state of perpetual astonishment; a book or a feather, a mouse or a fish or the dining-room table had all seemed equally miraculous, and I lacked the ordinary confidence in my own reality. I never went to bed without wondering what new shape I might inhabit by the morning. Almost from the beginning I was a disappointment to my parents. They had a position to keep up, and were ambitious too. They took it very badly when I was expelled from the school where my elder brother had been Head of his House and Captain of Cricket.

Now, after six years in the Army, I felt that I had served my apprenticeship to war, but I was still a novice in peace. So I couldn't, in honesty, set up as a teacher, and I had been looking for something else to do. I hadn't much to guide me except negatives. I didn't want to live in a town, for one thing, because I felt, at that time, the need to think; and peace to think, in my view of it, required the open sky.

I started badly, for after I had seen John Norquoy at a cattle market one day, I couldn't bring myself to go and tell him about Jim. I had wanted to make him, and all his friends, so proud of Jim that he would live for ever in their minds like a lighted lamp, to which their love would be as moths, gathering to his memory and beating its wings in the glow of him. Jim was my friend, and even the Seaforth Highlanders had never known a better man.

But when I first saw John Norquoy

I realised that it wasn't going to be easy to talk about pride to him, for he knew enough already. That was evident, though it was quite an ordinary occasion. He was looking at a thin-faced cattle-dealer pulling the loose black skin on the rump of a two-year-old heifer. There was nothing of the braggart in him, nothing loud or boastful, but he had the same build as Jim, the same sort of head ten years older, the look of a man who knew what he was after and what it was worth. He was smiling, and there was the same irony in his smile, though he was only selling a beast, as I had seen in Jim's face, grey with the strain of battle, when we had to withdraw from the Primo Sole bridge because our ammunition was spent, and the infantry who should have relieved us hadn't been able to get forward in time. There was nothing I could tell John Norquoy about pride, and when I realised that I put off going to see him. I put it off for about three weeks.

I stayed with the village school-master, a good man who had fought in the last war. I told him about my other difficulty, and he thought I could teach with safety in a country school. 'The children here,' he said, 'wouldn't worry you with awkward questions. They don't grow up with doubt in their minds. Life for them means birth and marriage and death, and they're all natural things. It means hard work and hard weather, and what amusement they and their neighbours can make for themselves. It means dancing and making love when they're young, and breeding a good beast and gossiping when they're older. And if, from time to time, they're troubled about the deeper significance of life, they keep their trouble to themselves. They know that it's an old trouble, and it wouldn't occur to them that you could cure it.'

But I didn't want to teach, either in country or town, so I spent my three weeks in idleness, but kept my eyes open. I had an open mind too, and no accomplishments. I was ready for suggestions; but not for going to see John Norquoy. I met Lydia one day, and talked to her for a quarter of an hour till her mother came out and called her in. The next time I saw her she had the gander with her, and she wasn't so friendly. I felt hurt and disappointed and a little angry, though I didn't realise then what she was really like. We pay too much attention to clothes, and hers were the sort you don't see in a town unless a strayed gipsy has come in. She had a small, beautifully shaped head, but her hair was tangled by the wind and greasy, and her features were so regular that I didn't notice, to begin with, how good they were. Her throat was lovely, long and as white as milk, but her neck was dirty, and when I saw her for the second time it was the same dirt, I'm fairly sure, that still darkened her skin. And yet I felt hurt when she wouldn't stay and talk to me.

I asked the schoolmaster about her, and he told me she was illegitimate, a state of being that's not extraordinary in country districts. Her mother was a grim old woman named Thomasina Manson, a crofter's only child, unpopular as a girl, who had lived a lonely and blameless life till she was about thirty-five, when she had gone to Edinburgh, and what she did there, except get herself into trouble, no one ever knew. It was generally supposed that she had been in domestic service, and when her baby was born, about three months after she came home, she told the doctor that its father came of the gentry. But that's all she told, and her father and mother, who had married late in life, never recovered from the shock. They were Plymouth Brethren, said the schoolmaster, sternly pious and pitiably dependent on their respect-ability. They died, one after the other, within a couple of years of Lydia's birth, and Thomasina was left alone to work the croft and bring up the child.

How, I asked, did she come to give it a name like Lydia?

The schoolmaster showed me a

register of the village children. About half of them had been christened simply enough: Thomas and James and Mary, Ellen and Jean and William and David, and a few of the girls had clumsy feminine trans-formations of masculine names such as Williamina and Davidina and – like Lydia's mother – Thomasina. But the rest were a fancy array of Corals and Dereks, Stellas and Audreys, and so forth. 'Their mothers take a fancy to names they've seen on the films or in a magazine,' he said. 'They don't suit our island surnames, but they produce, I suppose, the same effect in the house as a piece of new wallpaper or a set of new curtains. They seem bright and cheerful.'

A moment later he said, 'When are you going to see the Norquoys? They know who you are, and they're expecting you. But they won't ask you to come, they'll just wait.'

'It's not easy,' I said.

'It won't be as difficult as you think. They won't show any emotion, you needn't be afraid of that.'

'I'm thinking of myself,' I answered.

I waited another ten days, and then, one Saturday morning, I went to town – four thousand inhabitants and a little red cathedral – and managed to get a bottle of whisky. I arrived at the Norquoys' about six o'clock, and though I hadn't told them I was coming, they seemed to be expecting me. News travels quickly here, and even a man's intentions become public property as soon as he has realised them himself, and sometimes before. So I sat down to a mighty farmhouse tea in the kitchen, and no one said a word about Jim. They asked me what I thought of the islands, and where I belonged to, and if my parents were still alive, and they all laughed when I mistook a young sister of John Norquoy's wife for one of his daughters. There were ten or a dozen people at table, and I had to be told very carefully who they all were, and they thought it a great joke when I couldn't remember. But no one mentioned Jim.

After tea John Norquoy took me out to see the animals. He had a couple of fine young Clydesdales, a small herd of black-polled cattle, a great surly white boar, and a few score of sheep on hill pasture. We walked in his fields for a couple of hours, and still no word of Jim. But when we came back to the farm he led me into the benroom; a peat fire had been lighted in it, and going through the passage where I had hung my waterproof I took my bottle out of the pocket. Norquoy paid no attention to it when I set it down, but went to a little table in the window where another bottle, the same brand as my own, stood on a tray with glasses and a jug of water. He poured a couple of deep drams and said, 'It was very good of you to write about Jim in the way you did. We're most grateful to you, and we're glad to see you here. If you're thinking of staying, there's a bed for you when ever you want it.'

I took my drink before I answered, and then, slowly and little by little, I told him about Jim, and about the war, and what it means to go through five or six battles with the same friend beside you, and then to lose him in the last one. I realised, in an hour or two, that I was playing the bereaved brother myself, but I couldn't help it by then. Mrs Norquoy came in, and their eldest boy, and her sister that I had taken for Norquoy's daughter, and then two or three neighbours. I went on talking, and they listened. I got most of the load off my mind, and if they didn't realise, by the end of it all, that Jim had been a soldier, well, it wasn't my fault. And every word I spoke was the simple truth. But when I got up to go Mrs Norquoy said, 'We're peaceful folk here, Mr Tyndall, and Jim was one of us. How he endured all that fighting I just can't understand.' It wasn't till a few days later, when I remembered her words, that I began to realise how much they had disliked what I had been telling them. They were peaceful folk, and they didn't approve of war.

But at the time I wasn't in the mood to catch a fine shade of meaning. Both bottles were empty, and I had had a lot more than my share. John Norquoy drank moderately and showed no sign of having drunk at all. He had listened carefully, with little change of expression, and the questions he asked showed that he was following and remembering all I said. But he made no comments on my story. One of the neighbours liked his whisky well enough, but carried it as solemnly as a cask. I was the only one who seemed to have taken any benefit from what we had been doing, and Norquoy insisted on coming with me as far as the main road. I was walking well enough, but talking too much by then, and I told him – without difficulty – what I had been waiting for the strength to

30

tell. I got rid of the guilt on my mind.

For a black minute or two, splashing through the shallows of Commachio, I had been glad when Jim was killed. Glad it was he and not I whom death had taken, for we knew, both of us, that our luck was too good to last, and one or the other must go before the end. And when I saw it was Jim I was glad, and the guilt of it had lain on me ever since. Norquoy said nothing that I can remember, though I think he tried to comfort me and I know that he wanted to take me home. But I wouldn't let him.

Soon after we had said good night it came into my head that I would like to take a look at the goose girl's house. Lydia's, I mean. The last time I had seen her she had been driving her whole flock, fifteen or sixteen of them with the great gander in front like a drum-major, past a big shallow pool in the stream, where the cattle came to drink, and the whole procession had been reflected in the calm water as if to make a picture. To see her like that, in a picture, had made her more real – or am I talking nonsense? Ideal may be the word, not real. Anyone who's fit to be a teacher could tell you, and tell you the difference between them, but I'm not sure myself. But whatever the word should be, I looked at her on the other bank of the stream, she was wearing an old yellow jersey and a dirty white skirt and her legs were bare among the meadowsweet, and I looked at her reflection in the picture, and that night I dreamt of her, and in my dream she was trying to tell me something, but I couldn't hear her.

So I turned off the main road

towards her mother's house, and before I got there I realised how drunk I was. I'm not trying to excuse myself, but the whisky had been mixed with a lot of emotion, and as the result of one coming in and the other going out my knees were beginning to buckle, and when I came to the cottage I had one hunger only, and that was for sleep. There was a south-easterly breeze blowing, chill in the middle of the night, and to get into shelter I clambered over the garden wall, and the softness of the dug soil on the other side seemed very comfortable. I fell asleep under the currant-bushes, and what woke me was Lydia's screaming and the clattering of the gander's wings as she threw it out of the house.

Well, after I'd seen the bird go marching off, and disappear downstream, I went round, as I said before, to the lee-side of the cartshed and smoked a cigarette. I had been lying on the packet and they were pretty flat, but I rolled one into shape again, and while I smoked I thought, and came to a conclusion.

I fingered my chin, and it was smooth enough. I had shaved about five o'clock the afternoon before. I felt fresh and well. Sleeping on the ground had done me no harm, for I had grown used to that, and the night had been mild. My clothes were damp with dew and soiled with earth, but I took off my coat and shook it, and cleaned myself fairly well with some cut grass. Then I went down to the stream, and kneeling on the bank I washed my face and rinsed my mouth, and drank a few handfuls of water.

The door, the unlocked door, opened easily enough and I made no noise going in. I stood in a little passage with some old coats hanging on the opposite wall, and an uncarpeted wooden stair before me that led to a loft. To the right there was a door into the kitchen, where the old woman slept in a box-bed, and to the left was the ben-room with a closet on the inner side where Lydia slept. The ben-room door was closed with a latch, or a sneck, as they call it here, and my hand was steady. I opened the door without a sound, but only two or three inches, and looked in.

Lydia had put on a long white nightgown, an old-fashioned garment with coarse lace at the neck, and she was sitting at the north window, the one that opens into the yard. She held a looking-glass in both hands, and was staring at her reflection. Her right cheek – the one I could see – was pink.

She jumped up with a gasp of fear, a hoarse little noise, when I went in, and faced me with the looking-glass held to her breast like a shield. 'What do you want?' she asked, but her voice was quiet.

I closed the door behind me and said, 'If you had asked me that a week ago, I couldn't have answered you. I might have said *Everything* or *Nothing*. I didn't know. But that was a week ago.'

'What does that matter to me?' she asked. 'Why have you come here?'

'Because now,' I said, 'I do know.'

'You have no right to come into my room,' she whispered.

'I want you to marry me,' I said. 'I want a wife.'

She flushed and asked me, 'Why do you think you can find one here?'

Then I told her, or tried to tell her, why nothing had any force or weight in my mind, after seeing her as I had seen her that morning, but to live with her in the love of a man for his wife, in the love of possession without term or hindrance. She turned pale, then red again, when I said that I had seen her wrestling with the gander, and tried to push me out. But I caught her by the wrists, and spoke as a man will when he is wooing, in fumbling and broken words, of her beauty and the worship I would give her. Fiercely, but in a voice as low as a whisper still, she cried, 'I want no one's worship!'

'Last night,' I said, as urgently but as softly as she spoke herself – for the old woman was sleeping only a few yards away – 'Last night my mind was full of bitterness and grief. There had been little else in it for a year or more. But I emptied it, last night, and this morning you came into its emptiness and took possession. And I'm not going to live again like a man who's haunted. I'm not going to live with a ghost in my mind, with a ghost walking on my nerves as if they were a tight-rope, a ghost outside the window of my eyes and just beyond my fingers! I want reality. I want you, in my arms as well as in my mind, and I want the Church and the Law to seal you there.'

She answered nothing to that, and I went on talking, but I don't think she listened very closely, for presently she interrupted and asked me, 'Where did the gander go?'

'Down the burn toward the loch,' I told her.,

'That's where he came from. He came here about a month ago, and killed the old one. The gander we had before, I mean.'

'He won't come back,' I said. 'He's had enough of you, after the way you handled him.'

She turned to the window, the one that opens into the yard, and looked out, saying nothing. I went behind her and put my arms round her. She tried to push me away, but with no determination in her movement, and I talked some more. She listened to me now, and presently turned and faced me, and said yes.

The next morning I began my new life of work and responsibility. I bought a boat, a heavily built, round-bellied dinghy, ten-and-a-half-foot keel and in need of paint, for £18.10s. Two days later I took a summer visitor out fishing and made fifteen shillings for six hours' easy work. It was a good fishing loch, and there were visitors in the islands again for the first time since 1939. I could look forward to three or four days' work a week, and as trout were selling for 2s.9d. a pound I sent home for my own rod and tackle, and did quite well on my unemployed days in addition to enjoying them. I could have done still better with night-lines and an otter at dusk and a little caution, but I like fishing too much to cheat at it.

I was still living with the schoolmaster, for £2.10s. a week, but our relations became a little cooler when his wife discovered that I was sleeping out. That didn't worry me, however, for my happiness that summer was like the moon and the stars, shining and beyond the reach of malice.

It puzzled me a little that I couldn't persuade Lydia to settle a date for the wedding, as I thought there might be a proper reason for it before long, but when I once spoke of it more seriously than usual, she said, 'We're perfectly happy as we are. I don't see why we should bother. Not yet, at any rate. And I'll have to explain to mother, and she's difficult sometimes.'

'I'll do any explaining that's necessary.'

'No, no! You must leave that to me. You won't say anything to her, will you?'

I said I wouldn't. She asked very little of me – she never has asked much – and neither then nor now could I refuse her anything. She had made a good pretence of surrendering, but my surrender went deeper. I had become the roof and the walls within which she lived, but she was the soul of the house. I thought of

41

Jim whenever I looked up at the Kirk hill and saw Norquoy's farm on the slope of it, but to think of him didn't make me feel guilty now. I was no longer obsessed by him, and if a new obsession had taken his place, I had no cause to grumble against it. So June and July went quickly by in that happiness and in good weather, though not settled weather, for the island skies are always changeable, till one day in mid-August, when I came ashore in a rising wind, colder than it had been for weeks, the old woman met me and without a word of greeting said, 'You'd better come home to your tea.'

'That's very kind of you,' I said, and pulled the boat up and took out the two trout which were all I had caught. 'Would you like these?' I asked.

'It's a poor return for a day's

work,' she said, though they were good fish, the better one a little over the pound, and slipped them into the pockets of the old raincoat she was wearing without a word of thanks. She had a man's cap on her head, and boots like a ploughman's. We walked along the road together, not saying much, and tea was a silent meal but a good one. She or Lydia had newly baked bere bannocks and white bannocks, there was sweet butter and salt butter, and I ate a duck's egg and the half of a stewed cock chicken. Then, when we had finished, she said, 'Lydia tells me that you're wanting to be married.'

'It's what I've been wanting for the last two months and more,' I told her.

'She couldn't agree, and you wouldn't expect her to, until she'd spoken to her mother about it,' said the old woman grimly. 'She's a good girl, and it's a treasure that you're getting.'

I told her, humbly, that I was well aware of that.

'You've been a soldier, she says?'

'For six years I was.'

'I'm glad of that,' she cried, nodding her head. 'It's an ill world we live in, and there's times when the soldiers are all we can depend on, though it's a fool's trade if you look at it squarely.'

I had nothing to say to that, and she went on briskly: 'Well, if you're going to be married you'll be married in a decent manner, with the neighbours there to see it, and something good enough for them to remember too.'

'A wedding,' I said, 'is a woman's affair. I'm willing to be married in any way that suits Lydia. If she wants a big wedding, we'll have it. I've got about a hundred and sixty pounds in the bank —.'

'We're not asking you for money,' said the old woman. 'It's not a pauper you're marrying, no, faith! nor anything like poverty neither.'

She went to an old black wooden desk that stood in a corner of the kitchen, with a calendar pinned above it, and took a bank pass-book from a pigeon-hole stuffed with papers. 'Look at that,' she said, and held it open in front of me.

I was flabbergasted. It had never occurred to me that they could have any money at all, but the pass-book showed a credit of £1,207.

'Eight hundred and fifteen pounds of that is Lydia's own money,' said the old woman. 'Five hundred pounds came to her when she was born, and the rest is the interest which I've never touched and never shall. Her money will be hers to spend as she wants when she's of age – you've got three years to wait, so you needn't go to market yet – and the wedding I'll pay for out of my own.'

She gave me a dram then, and took one herself. Just the one each – it was the first time I had tasted whisky since that night at the Norquoys' – and then she put the bottle away in a cupboard with some fancy tumblers and glass dishes. She went out to the byre after that, to milk their two cows, and left Lydia and me together. Lydia had hardly spoken a word since I came in.

The following Sunday the banns were read in the Parish Church, and a few days later the old woman showed me the invitation cards she had had printed for the wedding. She hadn't done it cheaply, that was clear. They were a good thick board with gilt edges, and they read:

Miss Thomasina Manson
requests the pleasure of your company
at the wedding of her daughter
Lydia
to Mr. Robert Lacey Tyndall
in the Ladyfirth Parish Hall
at 6 p.m. on Wednesday, September 6th
R.S.V.P. *Dancing*

I said they had a very dignified appearance, and so they had if you weren't so hidebound by convention as to be startled by the prefix to the mother's name. The old woman was very proud of them, and propped one up on the chimney-piece. Then Lydia and I sat down at the kitchen table and began to write in names and address envelopes. The old woman had prepared a list, and there were two hundred and eighteen names on it. But by then I was beyond surprise.

I had no difficulty in dissuading my own parents from coming. I had always been the unwanted member of my family, and I had disillusioned them so often that they could guess the disappointment they would find in my wedding. They had grown accustomed to my disappointing them. I had never enjoyed teaching in an elementary school in Falkirk – that was due to my falling in love, at the age of nineteen, with a female Socialist with red hair and the sort of figure that, in a jersey, is like an incitement to riot – but they were shocked by my choice of a profession. They were less perturbed when, later, I went to sea as a deck-hand on a tramp steamer. They didn't like that, but they regarded it as an escapade. In comparison with the rest of the family I was, of course, an utter failure, for both my brothers had gone to Oxford and done well there, and my sister had married the junior partner in a highly regarded firm of stockbrokers. When Archie, my elder brother, was given an O.B.E. my father was much better pleased than when I got my D.C.M. Neither he nor my mother made any serious offer to come to the wedding. I used to get drunk, when I was younger, and once or twice I had caused them serious embarrassment, so I suppose they thought I should get high, loud, and truculent, and make a spectacle of myself. My father sent Lydia a dressing-case, for which she could discover no purpose at all, and me a cheque for £25. But he missed something by not coming himself.

The old woman wore a black dress that had belonged to her mother, and a man's cap. Not the old ragged tweed one she usually wore, but a new black one such as countrymen sometimes wear at a funeral. She sat in a high-backed chair beside the band, and it was easy enough to guess her thoughts. 'I bore my child without benefit of clergy or the neighbours' goodwill,' she was thinking, 'but my child, by God! will have all the favour and fair wishes that money can buy. My child will be wedded as well as bedded, and no one will forget it.'

And no one who saw her will forget Lydia that night. I realised that I still had things to learn, for though I had doted on her beauty, now I was humbled by it. By her beauty and her dignity. I stood beside her, while the Minister was reading the service, and felt like a Crusader keeping his vigil. The schoolmaster was my best man, though his wife hadn't wanted him to be, and I could hear him breathing, hoarsely, as if in perplexity. He ate little more than I did at supper, and I could eat nothing. I danced twice with Lydia, and the rest of the time stood like a moon-calf while people talked to me. But Lydia was never off the floor, and all night her mother, in the high-backed chair beside the band, sat with a look that was simultaneously grim and gloating.

There was a great crowd there, the fiddlers were kept hard at it, and the wedding was well spoken of. Nearly everyone who had been invited had come, and thirty or forty more as well. All the Norquoys were there, but John and his wife left about two o'clock. Before he went he said to me,

'I'm very glad that you've become one of us, and I hope you'll settle down happily here. You were a good friend to Jim, and if I can help you in any way, be sure and tell me.'

'There's no one can help me more,' I told him, 'than by wishing that as I am to-night, so I may continue.'

Lydia came to say good-bye to them while we were speaking, and after they had gone she said, 'Jim Norquoy was always my mother's favourite among the boys in the parish. She used to tell him that he mustn't be in a hurry to get married, but wait till I grew up and see what he thought of me before going farther afield.'

The schoolmaster came and asked her to dance, and I went outside. The hall was hot and men's faces shone as if they had been oiled, but the night air was cool. There was no wind and the sky was a veiled purple with a little haze round the moon. I could hear the slow boom and dulled thunder of the Atlantic on the west cliffs, four miles away. West of the cliffs there was no land nearer than Labrador, and for a few minutes I felt dizzy, as if I hung in space over a gulf as great as that. The old woman had meant to marry her to Jim, but Jim had died, and I had fallen heir to his portion. 'You won't find it easy to go back,' he had said, as if he knew that another fate would claim me. Nor had I gone back to my own country, but come instead to his, to do what I had to.

I remember sailing once, near Oban, in a little yacht I had hired, and getting into a strong tide and being carried swiftly past a rocky shore though the wind had fallen and the sail hung loose. The moon was pulling the tide to sea, and I was going with it. I was helpless in the grip of the moon, and I felt the excitement of its power. – The sensation came back to me as I stood outside the hall where the band was playing, and listened to the Atlantic waves, driven by the wind of invisible distant clouds to march against our cliffs. I was moon-drawn again, though I could not see my star. But I knew then that I had come north to the islands, though innocent of any purpose, to take Jim's place, who should have married her but had been killed instead. That was my doom; and I wanted no other. In a little while I went in again and saw the old woman. She was satisfied.

It was nearly seven in the morning when the wedding finished, with the drink done, the band exhausted, and the guests hearing in their imagination the lowing of their cows waiting to be milked. Lydia and her mother and I walked home together, and as soon as we arrived the two of them changed into old clothes and went out to the byre.

Her wedding, however, wasn't the only time when I saw Lydia well-dressed. She had gone to the town day after day, and bought clothes in plenty. Her more ancient garments were thrown away, and her everyday appearance was now smart enough by country standards. She told me one night that it was her mother who had insisted on her dressing like a scarecrow, and often enough wouldn't even let her wash her face for fear of bringing men about the house.

The weeks passed with nothing to spoil our happiness, and I got a job under the County Council, driving a lorry. The mornings and the evenings grew darker, and after a great gale had blown for three days from the north-west the winter came. It was cold and stormy, but after the wildest days the sky might suddenly clear for an evening of enormous calm with a lemon-coloured sky in the west and little tranquil clouds high in the zenith. After the harvest had been gathered and the cattle brought in, the country became strangely empty and its colours were dim. But I liked it. Wherever you stood you had a long view of land and water, and though the sky might be violent, the lines of the hills were gentle.

When I came home one evening about the middle of November, the old woman told me that Lydia wasn't well. There was nothing seriously wrong, but she would have to stay in bed for a few weeks, and she wanted her – the old woman – to make up a bed for herself in the ben-room. I would have to sleep in the loft.

'The doctor has seen her?' I asked.

'No,' said the old woman. 'I don't believe in doctors.'

I had a general knowledge that accidents might occur in pregnancy, but no precise information, and I couldn't make a physiological picture in my mind. I thought of blood and mortality, and the old woman saw that I was frightened.

'Don't fret yourself,' she said. 'She's not going to die yet, nor for many a long year to come. She'll be a brisk, stirring woman long after you're in the kirkyard.'

'Is it only rest that she needs?' I asked then, thinking vaguely of some anatomical bolt or washer that might have shaken loose, and needed immobility to re-establish itself.

'Rest,' said the old woman, 'a long rest and a lot of patience. Now go in and see her, but don't worry her with questions.'

Lydia was pale and she had been crying, but when I knelt beside the bed she put her arms round my neck and told me, as her mother had done, that I mustn't worry. And I didn't worry long. Two or three days, I suppose, and then it began to seem natural that she should have to stay in bed. I took to reading to her when I came home from work. My mother had sent a lot of things that belonged to me, including a box of books. I never had many books, I can't remember having had much time for reading when I was younger, but there were some good stories of adventure that I had enjoyed: *Typhoon*

and *The Nigger of the Narcissus, Kim,*
and *The White Company,* and
Trelawny's *Adventures of a Younger Son,*
Kidnapped, and *The Forest Lovers,* and
Revolt in the Desert, and so on. I've read
them all to Lydia at one time or
another, and she seemed to enjoy
them. I liked reading them again. It
was Conrad who was responsible for
my going to sea after I had had a year
of teaching in Falkirk, and couldn't
stand it any longer. I made three or
four trips to the Baltic and the
Mediterranean in tramp steamers,
and a voyage to Australia as a
steward in a Blue Funnel boat. But
when the war began I had had
enough of the sea, so I joined the
Army. Lawrence of Arabia may have
had something to do with that, or it
may have been Kipling.

Only one thing happened to annoy
me in the next two or three months,

and that occurred one morning when I was taking a load of road-metal to a secondary road we were patching, and drove past the old woman's cottage. It was a dark day, as dark as gunmetal, and the rain was blowing across country in blustering squalls. As I came near the cottage I saw Lydia crossing the road, leaning against the wind with a half-buttoned waterproof flapping round her, and a zinc pail on her arm. I pulled up hard and jumped out.

'Are you trying to kill yourself?' I shouted. 'You're supposed to be in bed, aren't you?'

For the first time since the morning when I'd seen her throwing the gander out of doors, she was angry. Her face seemed to grow narrower than usual, and her lips as hard as marble. She stared straight at me – her eyes are grey, with

sometimes a flash of blue in them –
and said fiercely, 'I can look after
myself. You go about your business,
and I'll take care of mine.'

'You're supposed to be in bed,' I
said again, stupidly and sullenly.
There were some eggs in her pail.
They had a hen-house across the road,
and she had been feeding the hens and
gathering what eggs the draggled birds
had the strength to lay in that weather.
'It's madness for you to be stooping
and bending and carrying buckets of
meal,' I said.

'I wanted some fresh air,' she said.
'I can't stay in bed for ever.

'Your mother ought to know better,
even if you don't. I'm going in to see
her,' I said.

'You'll do no such thing!' she
cried. 'You leave mother and me to
manage our own affairs. Don't you
interfere, or you'll be sorry for it.

And now go! Go, I tell you. You've got work to do, haven't you? Well, go and do it!'

She was ten years younger than I and a good head shorter, but her words came like the smack of an open hand on my face, palm and knuckles, this way and that, and I stepped back, muttering some limp excuse, and got into my lorry again. I brought her some oranges at night, that I'd bought from a sailor, and we said no more about it. But two or three days passed before she asked me to read to her again, and then for another six or seven weeks we were calm and happy, though the loft was a cold place to sleep in, and sometimes when the moon shone through the sky-light I woke up to see the rafters and their black shadows, and thought for a moment or two that I was still in the Army, making the best of it in a deserted farmhouse, and once I stretched out my arm to feel if Jim was beside me.

About the middle of February I began to worry about arrangements for her lying-in. Or, to put it more accurately, to worry because no arrangements had been made. I talked with the old woman, who wouldn't listen to me, or wouldn't listen seriously, but I didn't say anything to Lydia in case I should upset her again. And then, before we had come to any decision, I got a telegram from Edinburgh to say that my father had had a stroke, and would I come at once. Archie, my elder brother, was with some Government commission in Washington, and Alastair, the younger, was still in the Army in Rangoon. I didn't want to go, I had never got on well with my father, but the old woman said that if he died without seeing me I would be saddled with regret, like a heavy curse on me, for all the days of my life, and Lydia was plainly shocked, as if by the sight of some fearful wickedness, when I said that he could die as happy by himself as with me holding his hand. So, after a day of argument, I went to Edinburgh, and for a week my mother and I were uncomfortable in each other's presence, and my father slowly recovered. I had been wrong when I said that he wouldn't want to hold my hand. He did. I sat by his bedside for two or three hours every day, and sometimes, with a lot of difficulty, he managed to speak a few words. I was glad, then, that I had done what Lydia wanted. One day my mother told me that he meant to give me a present, and when I went upstairs he smiled and pointed to a leather case that lay on a chair beside him. It was his favourite gun, a fine piece by Holland, far too good for a man who lived in a cottage and drove a lorry for the County Council.

I said good-bye to them in a hurry when a letter came from Lydia to say that she had given birth to a daughter the day after I left her. 'I am very well and so is she,' she wrote, 'and I didn't want to disturb you with my news when you had so much to harrass you already. But now, if your father is no longer in danger, I hope you will be able to come home again.'

I said good-bye, but I didn't leave them for another fortnight. My father had a second stroke, and while I was sitting in the train and waiting for it to start, my sister came running along the platform, looking for me, to tell me I mustn't go. He lived for more than a week, but never regained proper consciousness, and then I waited for the funeral. I read Lydia's letter again and again, and two others that she wrote, both of which were full of news about the child. 'I think she may be the most beautiful baby in the world,' she said.

In my mind, when I saw her, there was no doubt at all. She had the perfection of a doll that some dead sculptor – a sculptor too great to be alive in this world – had carved in love from a rosy-veined alabaster. She was very small, and perfect. She was sleeping, and I had a monstrous fear that she might never wake. I put out my hand to touch her, but Lydia caught my wrist and shook her head. 'Let her sleep.'

I made no mention of something I found, a day or so after my return, for I couldn't be certain, then, that there was any meaning in it, and if there was I didn't want to think about it. The sight of it, in the grass, struck deep into my mind like a forester's wedge that splits the fibres of a tree, and for a minute or two I stood trembling. But there was no sense in it, and I didn't want to curse myself with a madman's doubt. I wanted to be at peace, and dote upon the child, so I denied the meaning of it and let it drown in the daily ebb and flow, the tidal waters of common life. It sank into the darker parts of my mind like a body into the deep sea with a sack of coal lashed to its ankles, as I had seen a sailor buried once. Committed to the deep, as they said.

The child grew quickly, and at six months she was like an Italian picture of a cherub, her head covered with small tight curls, paler than gold, and eyes the colour of a harebell. The old woman said she could understand already every word we said, and neither Lydia nor I was very serious about contradicting her. For we all thought of her in a way that I can't suppose is usual even in the fondest of parents. It wasn't only with pride of possession and a flood of affection whenever we looked at her, but with a kind of glee that never grew stale or sour in the remembrance of its excess.

In May I gave up my job but told the Road Surveyor that I should be glad to have it again in October. He wasn't too favourably disposed to my plans at first, but I had served him well, he was a fisherman himself and knew the compulsion of it, so after a little argument he agreed to let me go and take me back again when autumn came. I painted my boat, put my rod together, and had a week's fine sport before the first of the summer visitors arrived. Then, for three or four days a week till September, I watched my patrons fish, and calculated by the end of the September that my own average, on the intervening days, was about as good as the best of theirs. But I fished longer hours than they did, and the price of trout was still high.

Sometimes I used to wake up at night, with Lydia beside me, and see the darkness about us like the mouth of a huge engulfing fear. I had no right to be so happy. No one had such a right. It was like oil on the top step, it was like a German white flag with a sniper lying beside it, it was like a spider telegraphing *Walk-into-my-parlour* over his lethal gossamer. I would lie in the darkness, open-eyed, for perhaps an hour, drenched in fear, but in the morning, waking and turning to Lydia, and then playing with the child for half an hour, my happiness would come back like the returning tide. I couldn't help it. They were both so beautiful.

Once, when the child was about fifteen months old, I woke in the first phase of one of my frightened moods, and saw her standing up at the end of her crib. She had taken off her nightgown and she was poised with her head tilted up, her arms out and her hands resting on the siderails of the crib as if she were addressing a public meeting; or facing her judges, unafraid. There was a late moon that night, and though the window was small there was light in the room. But that wasn't the light that irradiated the child. Her light, unless I'm the simple victim of some cuckoo-born delusion, came from within. Now Lydia's body, on that first morning when I saw her throwing the gander out of doors, was gleaming like mother-of-pearl, or a pearl on velvet, with a light of its own; but never since then had I seen her better than a milky white. – As white as milk and as smooth as curds, but not with that radiance. – Yet now the child, naked in the darkness, was gleaming with such a light. It was no brighter than the moonlight dimmed by white curtains, but it wasn't in the overflow of moonlight she was shining. It was in a light of her own.

I slipped out of bed, quietly so as not to waken Lydia, and said to the child, 'You'll catch cold, standing up like that. You ought to be asleep.' She looked at me for a moment, as if surprised to see me there, and then twined her arms round my neck and kissed me. I put on her nightgown and obediently she slid down between the blankets.

A year went by and part of another. I came, I suppose, to take my good fortune for granted, and my happiness perhaps lost something of its fine edge and became a rounder contentment. Time, when I look back, seems to have gone very quickly and as smoothly as the water curving over a weir in a polished flow without break or interruption. We were on friendly terms with our neighbours, I saw the Norquoys and the schoolmaster every week or two, and gradually I came to think of the islands as my own place, my proper environment in which I had become an accepted part. But my real life was lived on the old woman's croft, at home. My senses were livelier there, my feelings more profound, my consciousness of life more widely awake.

The old woman could work as well as a man. She could plough and harrow, and between us, when harvest came, we cut and bound and stacked four acres of oats. Lydia looked after the poultry, and singled turnips, took her fork to hayfield and harvest, as well as doing housework and tending the child. We were rarely idle and often our work was hard, though I don't remember that we found it unduly hard because we did it all in our own time, and we had no master to drive us or reprove us or thank us. I couldn't spend so much time fishing as I had done when I first lived there, but I enjoyed working on the land so long as it wasn't continual work.

In the winter months, when I drove a lorry again, I used to read in the evenings. Both Lydia and her mother liked the tales of adventure best. I had some other books, by Jane Austen and Dickens and Galsworthy, that I had never read myself, but we didn't care for them. It was a tale of far-off lands, with the noise of a dangerously running sea, or the thud of a sword going stiffly home, the crack of a rifle, that the women liked. There was something fierce in them, an appetite for deeds, that couldn't show itself in their ordinary life, but was there all the time and came out of hiding a little when I read to them. But domestic scenes, and comedy and conversation, bored them.

Well, this good easy life continued – it wasn't physical ease that characterised it, not in those northern winters, but we were all contented – till the child was in her third year, and then one summer day when there fell a flat calm and the loch lay like a mirror, pocked with rising trout, but not one that would look at a fly, I came ashore at midday and on the road a little way past the house I saw five carts standing, three of them loaded with peat and two empty. The loaded ones, coming home from the hill, were John Norquoy's, and the horses between their shafts stood motionless, with drooping heads, their shoulders dark with sweat. The empty carts belonged to a neighbour of his who had started earlier and was on his way back to the hill for a second load. His horses were restless, tossing their heads and pecking at the road with steel-shod hooves. But their drivers paid no attention to them. John Norquoy and two others were squatting on their heels, on the road, and two were leaning against the nearest cart, and in the midst of them, her hands behind her back like a girl reciting poetry at a village prize-giving, was the child. She was talking, and they were listening.

I waited for a little while, some forty yards away, but none of them turned a head in my direction, and when I went up and spoke to them, some looked sheepish and embarrassed, but John Norquoy, still on his heels, said to me, 'I could wish you had stayed away and not interrupted us. It's a real diversion, listening to her.'

I picked the child up and asked her, 'What were you talking about?'

'I was telling them a story,' she said, and when I set her on my shoulder she turned and cried to them, 'Goodbye now!'

I don't fully know why, but this small incident annoyed me at the time of it and worried me later. I told Lydia and her mother what I had seen, and said they would have to take better care of the child, for I wasn't going to have her grow up to believe she must always be the centre of attention. I didn't like to see a child showing-off, I said. 'Perhaps,' I went on, 'we ourselves are to blame, for we've always made much of her – too much, I dare say – and let her see that we're proud of her. But we'll have to change our ways if they're going to have a bad effect.'

'We could change our ways a dozen times without changing her,' said Lydia.

'That's nonsense,' I said. 'A child is the product, very largely, of what she's taught. I used to be a teacher myself—.'

'The old woman interrupted me with a cackle of laughter. 'It would take more than you,' she said, 'to make an ordinary bairn out of that one.'

Then I lost my temper, and for the first time we had a proper quarrel. We had had differences of opinion before, and sometimes grown hot about them, but this was different. Now we grew bitter and said things to each other that were meant to hurt, and did. The argument didn't last long, but at night, when Lydia and I were alone, it flared up again. It was she who began it, this time, and when I saw that she was bent on making trouble – her face put on its fierce and narrow look, her lips were hard – I smacked her soundly on the side of her head, and before she could recover I laid her across my knee and gave her an old-fashioned beating with a slipper.

A week or two passed before she

forgave me. Or, perhaps, before she openly forgave me. I knew her fairly well by that time, and I don't think she bore a grudge against me for the beating, but because she didn't want to admit defeat she maintained an appearance of hostility till the affair could be regarded as a drawn battle. Then for a week or two we were in love again with a new fervour.

It was towards the end of February, a few days before the child's third birthday, that the gander came back, and I realised that fear of his return, an unregarded but persistent fear, like the white wound-scar on my leg that I never thought of unless I was tired or there came a hard frost, had always been with me.

There had been heavy snow, piled into great drifts by a strong wind, and for a few days work on the roads came to a stop and I had a winter holiday. The sun came out, the sky cleared to a thin bright blue, and the land lay still as death under a flawless white surface that gave to every little hill and hollow the suavity of ancient sculpture. The loch within a fringe of crackling ice, a darker blue than the sky, was framed in white, and a few swans like small ice-floes swam in a narrow bay. On land there was nothing stirring, and the smoke rose straight from the chimneys of diminished houses.

I had gone out with my gun – the fine piece by Holland – to try and shoot a late hare, and after following tracks in the snow for an hour or two I had got a couple. I was on my way home again when I saw, by the burnside a few hundred yards from the house, the child in her blue cap and her little blue coat. The burn, bank-high, was running strongly, and I hurried towards her with a sudden feeling, as of a man caught among thorns, of nervousness and annoyance that she should be there with no one to look after her.

She stood with her back to me, in her favourite position, her hands clasped behind her, and not until I had come within a few yards of her did I see the gander. He was afloat in a little smooth backwater of the burn, but as soon as he caught sight of me he came ashore, his broad feet ungainly on the snow but moving fast, and I thought he was going to attack me. The child turned and I called to her: 'Come here, Nell! Come here at once!'

But she stayed where she was and the gander came up behind her and opened his wings so that she stood by his breast within a screen of feathers as hard as iron and as white as the snow beyond them. It must have been the whiteness of the fields, with the bright haze of the sun upon them, that dazzled me and deluded me into thinking that the gander had grown to three or four times his proper size. His neck seemed a column of marble against the sky, his beak was bronze, and his black eyes reflected the sun like shafts from a burning-glass. A low rumbling noise, like the far-off surge of the sea on a pebble-beach, came from his swollen throat.

I'm not a coward and I couldn't have been frightened of a bird. It was snow-sickness, I suppose, that set my brain swimming and undid the strength of my knees, so that I thought I was going to faint. I remember seeing the same sort of thing happen to a soldier in Italy, in the mountains in winter-time. He was a friend of my own, a big fellow as tall as myself. He stumbled and fell, and the strength went out of him. We thought he had gone blind, but after we got him into a house and had given him some brandy, he was all right.

When I came to myself and knew what I was doing, I was on my hands and knees, crawling, and my hands were on fire with the friction of the snow. I had to crawl another twenty or thirty yards before I felt fit to stand up, and then I staggered and stumbled as if I were drunk. I wasn't far from home by then, and I rested for a while in the barn.

When I felt better I went into the kitchen. The child was there already, and as soon as I came in she ran towards me, and pushing me into a chair climbed on to my knee. She began to pat my face and play with my hair, as if trying to comfort me.

Presently I went out again, and found my gun and the two hares where I had dropped them. There was no sign of the gander. They were big hares, both of them, and I took them into the back-kitchen and got a basin, and cleaned and skinned them. But all the time I was thinking: Well, this is the end of pretence. There's no point or purpose in denial now. But what am I going to do?

The women were on the other side, so I couldn't talk to them. Lydia was in love with me, as I with her – there was no doubt about that – and the old woman liked me well enough; but now I knew the dividing-line between us, and I couldn't cross it. But I had to talk to someone.

John Norquoy wouldn't do. I had made a confession to him before, and it was too soon to make another. Nor would he believe me if I did. I had no great faith in the schoolmaster either, but I had to do something, say something to someone, and after tea I set out for his house, walking heavily through the snow, and if he was surprised to see me he didn't show it, but made me welcome. He had spent three or four idle days, with only a dozen children able to come to school, and in his own way he too may have been glad of a chance to talk for a while. His wife left us to ourselves.

I didn't know how to begin, but he helped me. He had been reading a book whose author was trying to prove that modern war was the result of conflicting demands for oil; and he, full of brand-new information, was ready to argue that war had always had economic causes, and no other causes. I didn't believe him, and said so. It was ideas that made war, I said. If an economist went to war, with material gains in view, it was because he was a bad economist, a quack and a charlatan; for any practical economist knows that war is likely to waste far more than it can win. 'But if men believe in ideas, of power and glory, or religious ideas, or even social ideas,' I went on, 'they may go to war for the simple reason that idealists don't count the cost of what they want. They go to war, that is, in despite of the economic arguments against it. And they're always against it.'

We talked away on those lines, getting warmer all the time, and the schoolmaster, really enjoying himself now, went back into history, back and back, till he had proved to his own satisfaction that the Peloponnesian War was due entirely to the imperialism of Athens, and the determination of the Athenians to brook no interference with their mercantile marine.

'And did Agamemnon and Menelaus,' I asked him, 'go to war to win the right of exploiting mineral resources in the windy plains of Troy?'

'If we really knew anything about the Trojan War,' he said, 'we should probably have to admit that that indeed was the cause of it; or something very like that.'

'It's not the generally accepted cause,' I said.

'According to the fable,' he answered, 'the purpose of the war was to recover, from the person who had carried her off, the erring wife of Menelaus. And who was she? Zeus, who never existed, is said to have visited a fictitious character called

Leda in the guise of a swan, and the result of their impossible union was a legendary egg out of which a fabulous being named Helen was incredibly hatched. Helen, says the story, grew to miraculous beauty, married Menelaus, and ran away with Paris. You can't seriously regard a woman who wasn't even a woman, but only a myth, as the cause of a war.'

'It lasted for ten years,' I said.

'I've been talking history,' he said. 'You really shouldn't try to answer me with mythology.'

'How does a myth begin?' I asked.

'How does a novelist go to work?' he demanded.

'By drawing on his experience, I suppose.'

He got up immediately and fetched a bottle of whisky and two glasses from the sideboard. Then he went out for a jug of water, and when he came back I said, 'What's worrying me is this. If a man discovers something within the scope of his own life that will eventually be a cause of war between nations, what can he do about it?'

'What could such a thing be?' he asked.

'I can't explain.'

'But it's impossible,' he said. 'War hasn't a simple origin or a single cause that you can take in your hand like a trophy to be fought for in a tournament. You have to consider the whole economy of the rival countries, their geographical situation, the growth of their population –.'

'And their ideas,' I said. 'Their leaders' desire for power, or a new religion, or a woman.'

'You're going back to your myth,' he said.

'You fought in one war, I fought in another. My experience of war is that you fight for five years, and at the end of it you see your best friend killed beside you, and you're glad – you're glad, by God! – that it's he who's dead, and not you. I don't want another war.'

'Well,' he said, 'whatever starts the next war, it won't be a woman. You can put that fear out of your head.'

'I'm not so sure,' I said.

The argument went on for a long time, and gave me no satisfaction. But talking did me good, and we drank a lot of whisky. When I got home I felt calmer, but very old, as if I were a character in a Greek play who saw the enormous tragedy that was coming, and could do nothing but wait for it, and then abide it.

Lydia and her mother were in bed, and I got a lantern from the back-kitchen. I lighted it and went to the stable. Meg, the old black mare, was twenty-seven or twenty-eight, and we dared not let her lie down in her stall for fear she could never get up again, so every night I put a broad canvas sling under her belly, to take the weight off her legs, and she slept standing. She woke as I went in, whinnying softly, and turned her head to watch me.

I stood on a wheelbarrow in the empty stall beside her, and reaching to the top of the wall, where the rafters go in, took down what I had hidden there, and never looked at since, nearly three years before. I had made a parcel of it, with string and brown paper, and now it was covered with thick cobweb. I brushed off the web and cut the string. For a moment or two I held in my hands the cigarette-box – covered with a fine Florentine leather stamped in gold, that I had taken from one of those little shops on the Ponte Vecchio – and then I opened it.

Inside lay the broken shell of a big white egg. I fitted the larger fragments together, and judged it to have been about seven inches long and rather more than four inches in diameter at the widest part.

That was what I had picked up, after coming home from my father's funeral, in the long grass under the ben-room window. It may seem funny to you, but you're not in my position.

THE DREAMING BEARS

THE DREAMING BEARS

In the Art Gallery at Abo there is a picture of a Finnish peasant by Gallén-Kallela. It was painted in the 'eighties, I suppose, under the influence of French naturalism. There is some reminiscence in its manner of Bastien-Lepage, but the subject belongs sternly, and sadly, and beautifully to the artist's own country.

It is the woman's hands that first compel attention. Gnarled and bent and discoloured by the earth to which she belongs, they are not quite

95

human. The nails and the knuckles are as hard as a bear's claws, and the plumpness of their muscle is no softer than the pads of a bear's foot. But one of the hands, in a stiff ungraceful offer of affection, comes forward invitingly to a half-grown cat that crouches, with a hint in its posture of the untamed forest, on the bright spring grass at the woman's feet. Her feet, discoloured like her hands, are naked, and their small bent toes are prehensile, as if the earth were a great branch on which she balanced.

In her eyes there is a light that comes, one must believe, from some inward warmth, from the same shy unaccustomed yearning for affection that thrusts out her hand. A yearning that moves in her like an old and rusty spring. But her wrinkled face is so indurate with years of hardship that it can show no expression of love, and within their puckered lids her eyes are so small that they seem, to a passing glance, more cunning then tender.

How old is she? The skin upon her broad cheekbones is tough as leather, and the wrinkles about her mouth are like crevices in a heavy soil that the sun has cracked. By her face she might be sixty, but her body is too round for so many years, and with a shock one sees that she is pregnant. A certain revulsion follows the shock, for the child in that sullen body can have been begotten only by some brutish rage stirring blindly in winter darkness. There is no place, one says, in that dull mind for the tenderness of love, for the questing and the agonies of love, for love that seeks a fulfilment of beauty amid doubt and torment, with gaiety and despair. Between that body and the neckless, broad, bow-shouldered body of its mate, what was there of love's delight? A winter rage, hunger in the dark. Nothing more – unless such creatures dream.

'The Finns are bears,' said my Swedish friend Bergström. 'If you understand that, you will find them quite tolerable. But be careful. Being bears themselves, they are capable of supposing that other people are the same. And if, indeed, you are not a bear, it is unpleasant to be treated as such.'

'But Gallén-Kallela was a Finn,' I said, 'and some of the other pictures by Finnish artists were very good too. And Sibelius?'

'They are quite clever,' he admitted, 'and certainly they have their dreams. But a bear is far from stupid, and he also dreams, it may be. He sleeps long enough and is fond of honey. And the mother-bear will lick her cubs to improve their appearance.'

I turned up the collar of my coat and shivered slightly. We had left the gallery and were walking along a rather dismal road on which the mud, but lately thawed, was beginning to freeze again.

'This is a bad time of year to visit Finland,' said Bergström. 'In the summer it is a very beautiful country, and in midwinter you would believe in magic. The air is like crystal, you feel very small to be walking in so clear a light. And in the north, during the night, there are great flames in the sky. But in the north, naturally, it is cold. I was serving with the Finns as a volunteer in their Winter War, and it was very cold. Once, I remember, we were waiting for something to happen, and I thought I was going to die, because it was so cold. We were waiting beside a wood, in the afternoon before it grew dark, and to the west the sky was pale green above a white hill. There was one cloud in it, a thin brown cloud like a crocodile with its belly shining red above the sun which had newly set. I thought I was dying, and the crocodile was like a real one. But then I heard a little noise, like dry twigs snapping, and I became afraid for another reason.'

'A Russian patrol?' I asked.

'After a fashion, yes,' said Bergström. 'But they were dead, of course. There were two of them lying beside us, they were frozen hard. And to amuse himself, the Finnish soldier who was with me was breaking their fingers. They went *snap!* and he laughed. "It is like the twigs breaking under the feet of an old witch who comes walking slowly through a wood,'' he said; and broke another finger to show me. He was telling himself a fairy tale, I suppose.'

I shivered again, and inclined slightly towards Bergström to avoid a man approaching us who seemed intent on keeping the middle of the road. He was a short burly man, pale of face and hard of jaw, with straw-coloured hair showing untidily under his cap. There was no one else near us, but as we passed he collided with me, and I staggered against Bergström.

'That is what they are like,' he said. 'Sometimes it is useful, and sometimes not. In warfare they are extremely brave, but even in the wilderness two Finns could not pass without bumping into each other. It is traditional. That is how their great poem begins, the Kalevala. You have read it?'

'I'm afraid I haven't.'

'Your Queen Victoria curtseyed when she received her poet Tennyson,' he went on, 'and in like manner everyone and everything in those days, the days of the heroes of the Kalevala, bowed low before the power of music, and were submissive to it. It is interesting to find, in a national epic, that the principle character is an old minstrel. His name is Vainamoinen. The names of all the people in the poem seem quite uncouth when you first hear them, but you quickly get used to them. Vainamoinen's young brother is the second hero. His name is Ilmarinen, he is a smith. And of course there is a heroine, a girl of great beauty, but unreliable. She does not let herself suffer because of love, or patiently endure long absence from her sweetheart, as a romantic heroine would. She is, on the contrary, extremely selfish, never to be satisfied, and in conclusion she is eaten by wolves. The poem is not by any means a romance, it is a fairy tale; and some of it is highly fanciful, and other parts are realistic.'

'And it begins, you say, with a head-on collision?'

'That is not the absolute beginning. The creation of the world comes first, of course, and that is effected, with more economy than usual, by breaking a duck's egg. The lower part of the shell becomes the earth, the upper half the sky, the golden yolk is the sun, and the white the moon. And then, when life has become properly established, the young minstrel Joukahainen drives out in his sledge to challenge old

Vainamoinen to a duel of singing. He encounters Vainamoinen, also in a sledge, and runs into him in the traditional manner of one Finn meeting another. That is his way of introducing himself. And in the contest that follows, Joukahainen is badly beaten, for old Vainamoinen sings the runners of his sledge into trees, and his whip to a reed in the lake, and his horse to a stone. He sings Joukahainen's sword into a flash of lightning, his arrows into hawks that soar above him, his dog into another stone. He sings Joukahainen's clothes off him, he sings him into a swamp, and buries him in it as deep as his nose. For such is the power of music.'

' "Orpheus with his lute made trees . . ." ' I began, but Bergström interrupted: 'Orpheus had nothing on old Vainamoinen! There was a famous occasion when Vainamoinen made a harp out of the bones of a great pike, and when he played upon it the birds and the fishes all hurried to listen, mermaids and clouds gathered round him, bears came lumbering over the fields and sat upon the fences, and when the fences broke they climbed into trees, which were bending forward and listening with great eagerness also. The music was so beautiful that presently everyone was weeping with joy, old Vainamoinen himself crying more copiously than anyone. His tears were bigger than cranberries, larger than peas, heavier than the eggs of a willow-grouse. Five wollen cloaks and ten overcoats became soaking wet with his tears.'

I pulled my muffler higher on my neck and knotted it more tightly to keep out the cold. The formless grey sky, the colour of old ice in the harbour, had split and parted in the west to show beyond it a clear enchantment of green vacancy, the colour of a duck's egg with a golden sun inside it. Of the broken eggshell that had made the firmament – or the eyes of the woman who had told me I should be killed?

I had crossed the Gulf of Bothnia, from Stockholm to Abo, in the strangest manner, having been a day and a night at sea without noticing water. The gulf was frozen from shore to shore and snow had lately fallen, thickly covering the sea-ice, so that we ploughed with a roar like gunfire, a growling of fretted floes, a rumbling interrupted by thuds and jars, through a blanched illimitable prairie dazzled by the sun. We opened a lane through the ice and left behind us a tumbled furrow; and talked to each other – for the ship was crowded – above the rending, cracking, roaring din. I was sitting in the saloon with some Swedes I knew, and two or three Finns with whom they were friendly. One of the latter was a young woman with a broad calm brow, a finely sculptured jaw, and cheekbones that her white skin lay smoothly on, smooth and tight, with never a wrinkle in it. Her eyes were a pale bright green with curiously small pupils.

I was speaking, idly in the way one does aboard ship, of my late visit to Sweden, of eating and drinking and talking till the morning came. 'Such hospitality!' I said. 'I nearly died of it.'

'In Finland,' said the woman with the green eyes, 'we shall make no mistake. We shall certainly kill you.'

There was nothing in that, of

course. It was a joke, quite a formal little joke. But, on the other hand, there was nothing in her voice, no movement in her expression, to show it was a joke. No wrinkle of laughter crossed the smoothness of her face, no shadow of amusement spoiled the transparency of her sky-green eyes. She looked at me calmly, unblinking, and I wondered a little uneasily if they still bred witches; and if it would be thought unmannerly to resist a spell.

The torn sky, green in the west, was the very colour of her eyes, and Bergström and I, having climbed to the old cathedral of St. Henry, stood in the porch to look at it.

'From what I have been telling you,' he said, 'you may suppose that the Kalevala is only a collection of tall stories. But you are wrong, I assure you. It is much more than that. There is sorrow in it, and betrayal, and perseverance, and mockery, and other human things. There was, for instance, a girl called Aino, whose mother had persuaded her to marry old Vainamoinen, though Aino was unwilling because of his great age. But one day when Aino was swimming in the lake, and climbed on to a rock to rest herself, the rock sank beneath her and she was drowned. Then her mother, in the extreme of grief and especially regretting her intention of marrying Aino to an old man whom she did not love, sat down to weep; and her tears, as you might expect, became three mighty rivers; and the rivers, as anyone could guess, descended in three great waterfalls; and in the middle of each waterfall stood a rock, and from the rock grew a birch-tree, and in the branches of the tree –

this, I think, you would *not* anticipate – on every tree a cuckoo sang. The first cuckoo sang to the drowned girl, mocking her, and cried "Sweatheart, Sweetheart!" The second cuckoo mocked old Vainamoinen, who had loved poor Aino, singing "Bridegroom, Bridegroom!" And the third cuckoo, cruellest of all, mocked the weeping mother. "Joyful!" it sang, "Joyful!" '

'The bears of Finland,' I said, 'are no ordinary bears.'

'They are cunning,' Bergström agreed. 'In the winter they have plenty of time to meditate.'

We went into the cathedral and were accosted by an old and lonely woman of the poorest sort, who had evidently been lying in wait for a chance visitor. She came to meet us with a beggar's outstretched hand. But it was a shrinking gesture, she was a reluctant beggar, and strangely like the peasant woman in the picture by Gallén-Kallela, though her hand was thinner and her feet were shod. But in her narrow wrinkled eyes there was the same small light: imploring tenderness, reflecting guile, or simply transparent to sorrow? – Oh, why seek other causes? There was sorrow enough, in Finland after its wars, to give everyone his ration of it.

The church was dignified, even handsome in a gaunt, unhappy way. It had seen better times. On the vaulted roof of a narrow aisle there was the faded remnant of painting that in its day had been intricately patterned, elegant. We struck matches to look at it, for by now the evening was growing dark.

'In three months from now,' said Bergström, 'everything will look quite different. It is a country that requires its summer. The birches are indescribably lovely, it is possible to fall in love with a birch-tree, and they have thousands of lakes to wave their branches to. The people are also more gay in summer. They come out in the sun. I mean, like flowers they come out, though in appearance of course they are by no means like flowers; especially the men, who have no necks.'

We were entertained to dinner at night, a dinner of forty people, and that was hardly less wonderful than the miraculous draught of fishes; for the whole country was sore with hunger. There was neither bread nor meat nor milk, in the ordinary way, and there would have been no coffee but for acorns. There was a Black Market, of course, for those who had any money – who were not many –

and friends from Sweden brought parcels of food whenever they came. Our companions ate their dinner with the solemn pleasure of well-behaved children when a Christmas-tree is plucked; and afterwards they sang.

The woman beside me had a high, light, very pleasant voice, and between the songs she told me what they were about. They had simple themes and rural scenery.

'It is nature that inspires all our poetry,' she said. 'In the Kalevala also – but perhaps you do not know our national epic?'

'I've heard a lot about it lately,' I said. 'An uncommon lot about it.'

'I like to think of it nowadays, because the heroes never let themselves be defeated. Old Vainamoinen, and Ilmarinen the smith, and Lemminkainen who is so reckless: they never give in. But some of it is quite childish, I suppose. I wasn't going to talk about it, only to say that, although it is a great poem, all its images are natural and simple and many of them even homely. When Ilmarinen the smith has a bath, for instance, he washes himself till he is as clean as a hen's egg. But that is not quite typical of the poem, I do not mean that. What is typical is the way the poet speaks about the forest and the lakes, the darkness and the sun and the wind.'

'How interesting, I began, 'for Sibelius –.'

'You mean his Fourth Symphony?' she interrupted. 'The Fourth Symphony in A minor? That is the music of nature, is it not? But it must sound very strange and mysterious if you do not know Finland, because it is entirely Finnish. It has no other influence but the scenery and the nature – yes, the whole nature – of our beautiful poor country.'

Our neighbours on either hand had heard the name, and three, four, five of them invaded our conversation. Sibelius had finished his new symphony, said one. He had destroyed all his manuscripts, said another. He had written a whole cycle of work that no one had ever heard, he had done nothing for many years, he had taken an oath, his heart was broken, he was old and spent, he was imperishable in age like a great oak-tree. – So the talk went to and fro, contradictory, fabulous: like talk of a hero in the prime of the centuries. Somewhere in the south of Finland he lived in seclusion, very old and famous in his long silence. Like a northern wind, stormy and white with rime but sweet as honey in a bear's paw, tough as the birch-trees bending in a gale, magical, lonely as Ukko the Creator when he walked in his blue stockings to the edge of the clouds to look for the sun and the moon – so his music had gone round the world, and his name, like a hero's of the past, had gathered fable and exaggeration. They gave him a hero's temper, a hero's appetite. He drank three bottles of claret after breakfast, they said, and six bottles after supper.

Then they sang again, a wild and melancholy song to an air of valiant sorrow. They had no meat nor milk nor bread, and coffee only by the oak-tree's bounty. Every family in the land had lost its sons in war, and now the conqueror was pillaging with cold efficiency. They slept in paper sheets, and in their stoves the fire was out. But music had not lost its power of metamorphosis, music could dispatch the dark, and they were like bears indeed in their enduring strength. They had their dreams that none could pillage, and in the south, in a house hidden by the forest, their old hero lived in the memory of his music, and from fantastic beakers – may Ukko keep his cellar full! – drank his three bottles of claret after breakfast, his six bottles after supper. Old Vainamoinen.

JOY AS IT FLIES

JOY AS IT FLIES

She has given beauty a new category, he thought, for she appears to be edible. She is the word made fruit, rather than flesh, and with sugar and cream she would be delicious. Her neck would taste like an English apple, a pippin or nonpareil, and her arms, still faintly sunburnt from the mountain snow, of greengages.

'How old are you?' he asked.

'Nearly nineteen,' she answered, 'and I'm very mature for my age. We had lectures on all sorts of things at Lausanne. Really up-to-date lectures on genetics, and Cocteau, and the ballet, and – oh, everything!'

'And what's your opinion of Cocteau?'

'Well, I don't think the lecture on him was a very good one – what are you laughing at?'

'I'm sorry.'

'I never pretended to know *much* about him, did I? But I do know who he is, and what he is, and that's something.'

'It's a great deal.'

'Then you shouldn't have laughed at me.'

'You make me feel light-hearted: that's the trouble.'

'You mustn't be light-hearted about the match, or everybody will be furious. A Rugby International is very serious.'

They stood idly, in a moving throng of people, in the cold sunlight of March in Edinburgh. If they should step over the sharply drawn line between light and shadow, into the shadow of the tall stand, the darker air would be as cold as January. But the several thousands of people, hearty and red of cheek, who were streaming into the ground to see a match between England and Scotland, thought their northern climate could not be bettered. They brought their own warmth, a genial excitement, a general euphory that made men's voices ring louder and more kindly than usual and girls look vivid and pretty though they were not.

Latimer, when he woke that morning after a night in the train, had had no expectation of watching Rugby football. His mind had lately been occupied by a domestic issue of the greatest importance, and he had come unwillingly to Edinburgh on business that could not be postponed or delegated. For nearly two hours he had argued stubbornly with an elderly and cantankerous Writer to the Signet who, having got his way with most of the disputed clauses, became suddenly jovial, insisted on taking Latimer home with him to a luncheon-party of ten people, and there persuaded him, easily enough, to go to the match. There were seats for all of them, but in different parts of the stand: two quartets and a pair.

'Latimer,' said the crusty old man, mellowed now by food and a second glass of port, 'your're an Englishman and England's going to be beaten. But you're my guest, so we'll need to provide you with pleasure of some kind. You'll take Corinna, and sit with her ...'

'Oh look!' she exclaimed, catching his arm and pointing to an ancient victoria, a shabby survival of carriage-days, that on creaking wheels rolled slowly towards them. It was drawn by a thin brown horse with enormous chestnuts depending from the inner faces of its large flat knees, and the cabman, in a greenish bowler and a short fawn-coloured coat, was small and old, pale of cheek but pink of nose, with a long unhappy upper lip. Three young men, who had done themselves too well at lunch-time and now regretted their extravagance, got hurriedly down, embarrassed by the attention they had attracted, and after quickly paying the cabman went off to their seats. The cabman, sour and dispirited, sat with the reins loose in his hands, and made no move to turn and go. The brown horse hung its head, and the pale sunlight showed the dust that lay thick upon the faded blue upholstery of the old carriage.

'Isn't it heavenly?' said Corinna. *How* I wish we could go for a drive!'

'There's nothing to prevent us,' said Latimer.

'There's the match. Uncle Henry would be livid if we missed it. We can't miss the match, can we? But it would be fun!'

'You can look at footballers every winter for the rest of your life; but cabmen are dying out.'

'So a carriage-drive might be an historic occasion?'

'It might.'

'You don't want to see England beaten. You're trying to escape.'

'That may be the reason. Or it

may be the light-heartedness I spoke of before.'

'We can't really go, can we? – Oh, he's driving away! Shout to him!'

'Cabby!' shouted Latimer.

'Where to?' asked the old man as the carriage tilted, the springs protested, they got in, and dust rose from the stained blue cushions to meet them.

'I don't think it matters.'

'Drive to the Castle,' said Corinna, 'and stop on the Esplanade. There'll be a view to-day. – Oh, isn't this the most wonderful thing that's ever happened?'

'I'm not quite sure how it did happen. I'm not sure if it should. Do you think, perhaps, that we ought to go back? Your uncle –.'

'Must we?' she asked.

She had leaned heavily against

him as the cabman wheeled abruptly on to a main road, and an antic fear had momentarily possessed him that he could not refrain from taking her into his arms and embracing her, regardless of the many latecomers to the match, now hurrying past on either side, who were already looking over their shoulders with amused or curious glances at the ancient carriage and its occupants so strangely going the wrong way. The impulse had seemed, for an instant, beyond control, and very properly it had frightened him. Only forty-eight hours before he had been sitting at his wife's bedside, his hands gripped fiercely by hers in her recurrent torment, and in his anxiety he had offered to the future all manner of extravagant bargains if she and her baby should survive their peril and their pain. For Latimer was in love with his wife, a lively black-haired girl, and the composure of his love was alarmed, as if a volcanic pulse had shaken it, by so urgent and unruly a desire to close with a young stranger. His conscience was perplexed, and over its surface ran the ruffle of fear lest he make an exhibition of himself. It was bad enough to be seen riding in a victoria, absurdly seated in an absurd vehicle trundling away from the football-ground that everybody else was moving towards; but to be caught embracing a girl, a lovely and seemingly edible girl of eighteen, under the bright intolerant sky of Edinburgh – oh, madness! Disaster shook its panic finger, goblin-eyed.

Out of his fear, then, he suggested going back, but when Corinna reproachfully asked, 'Must we?', he looked at her lips, become suddenly

childish, and the blank disappointment of her gaze; and brusquely
commanded his emotion. It was
trivial enough, he found, he could
rebuff it. As firmly as if fear had
been a ball in a squash-court
bouncing to his forehead, he drove it
from him and said confidently, 'I was
only thinking of your uncle – of my
rudeness to him – but we shan't be
missed, I'm sure. And you can see an
International next year.'

'I've been taken to football
matches ever since I can remember,
and to go for a drive instead . . . .'
She turned and waved her hand to
three small boys who whistled
derisively from the pavement-edge.
'They're jealous,' she said. 'Everybody is jealous of us. Look at that
deadly-dull woman leaning out of a
window! Oh, what dull lives people
lead! There ought to be more horses

in a town, they smell so beautifully.'

On the causeway-stones the wheels rattled, the hooves of the thin brown horse beat in steady rhythm an old-fashioned tune, and leather loosely slapped its hide. When the off-wheels were caught in a tram-line the carriage lurched and threw Latimer and Corinna close together, but in the same moment her attention was taken by a seagull, come inland from the Forth, that balanced solemnly on the rim of a large gilded mortar over the door of a chemist's shop; and he, having snubbed the panic impulse, now dreaded no mischance but felt stirring in his mind a high non-sensical pleasure.

'There are more dull people,' she said as they passed two women in respectable drab clothes, one of whom was old, and a narrow-shouldered man of depressed appearance. 'I couldn't bear to be middle-aged! I couldn't bear to be anyone else!'

'Some of us have our compensations,' he told her.

'Oh, but you're different.'

'Though it's true that many are unlucky. I once heard a man say, "I never got much fun myself, but some of my friends have had an amazingly good time."'

'How terribly sad!'

'So it seemed to me, but he didn't think so. He was a well-fed, apparently contented person.'

'But how could he be?'

'You don't know what secrets he had. You don't know anything about other people. You don't know what terrible strands of interest hold together those two dowdy women and the man with bottle shoulders.'

'Do you?'

'They may have a plot to strangle him after supper tomorrow, while he has a better plan to hit them on the head, with a stone in the toe of a stocking, after tea.'

'That's not typical of life in Edinburgh.'

'But you can't deny the possibility. You can't even tell me what the seagull saw that was sitting on the edge of a golden mortar outside a chemist's shop.'

'Do you think there was anything in it?'

'A rag and a bone and a little wooden box.'

'What was in the box?'

'The telephone-number of an old man who's forgotten what nobody else ever knew.'

'Goodness! You have got good eyes. Now tell me what he's looking at.' She pointed to a sailor who was staring into a fishmonger's full window.

'It can only be one thing, can't it?'

'Something horrible?'

'I'm afraid so. There's a flounder on the slab with his dead wife's ring in its mouth.'

'What a shock for the poor man! But perhaps she was a bad woman?'

'The worst woman in the world.'

They drove past houses set back from the road behind little gardens emptied by the winter, and looked at black or curtained windows, and the sky above them was as clear and cold as a great zircon. The old carriage groaned and rattled, and tall tramcars swaying on their shallow rails went shrilly past. Here and there, idly, Latimer read the name of a street: Roseburn, a shepherd's lyric deafened by stone, the remote Victorian echoes of Kew Terrace and

Osborne Terrace, then a flour-mill and the vanished rural chaffering of the Haymarket, and so into shabbier thoroughfares till they saw mounting high and precipitous before them the darkly gleaming Castle rock. And all the way they spoke of nothing grave, of no material subject, and little even of themselves but for Corinna's recollection, now and then, of some ludicrous girl at school or a mistress's peculiar discipline and her outwitting. Latimer talked nonsense with an imagination as fluent as a hill-stream after rain – or a fortune-teller's patter in a booth – and Corinna's voice, like a swallow hunting evening flies, went to and fro in effortless arcs and charming cadences after topics so minute as almost to be invisible. But subsequently, when Latimer tried to remember what subjects had held them in conversation, he was inclined to believe that somehow they had touched – oh, lightly, it is true, but with conscious fingers – eternal

themes and the poets' deeper chords.

He had made a joke about Byzantium – the architects of Edinburgh have sometimes had unlikely motives – but was it all a joke? He had described his sailing to the Fastnet in a leaking yacht improvidently manned, and made of dangerous misadventure a ludicrous tale; but surely in its burden had been the immemorial menace of the estranging sea? Corinna, talking of a

concert solemnly attended by twenty
schoolgirls, had described a plump
and bespectacled friend's untimely

woe, whom Gluck's *Orpheus* remind-
ed that she had not prepared her
necessary twenty lines of the Aeneid,
Book IV, which they were reading –
and then, oh surely then! they had
fallen silent to think of Queen Dido
in eternal grief upon the Africk
shore. Such notes they had struck, he
was sure of it in after years, though
honesty could find no certain words
to substantiate his faith. But a
vibration of remembered light suf-
fused his memory, as of goldfinches'

wings above a thistle-field in the sun; and a sonorous echo of emotion, like a bell at sea, kept it alive.

They drove slowly up Castle Hill, and leaving the victoria on the Esplanade climbed to St. Margaret's Chapel and looked northward over the Forth to the lands and the hills of Fife, dove-grey and glinting with gold. Corinna was confident of her geography and told him where the Bonny Earl of Moray had been slaughtered on the sea-wet rocks.

'Physical beauty was very rare in earlier times,' said Latimer. 'Beauty needs good food, and our ancestors fed poorly or foolishly. And because beauty was so rare it inspired a romantic devotion, while nowadays our appreciation is aesthetic –.'

'Is it?' asked Corinna.

'Yes, I believe so. And aesthetic appreciation –.'

'Is a little bit bogus, isn't it?'

'I don't think so.'

'Well, you're not really good-looking, but I like you.'

'I'm very glad. But are you being logical?'

'Oh, logic doesn't affect *people*!'

Slowly they walked down to the Esplanade again, and climbed into the waiting carriage. 'We'll be in Murrayfield before the match is over,' said Latimer. . . .

That was ten years ago, and he had not seen her since. War had invaded their uneasy climate, and Latimer, going to France in 1939, had retired hurriedly from Dunkirk a few months later, and served thereafter, sometimes dangerously on the field and sometimes in the mingled strain and camaraderie of a Divisional Headquarters, in North Africa and Italy. He had been more fortunate than many. He had recuperated pleasantly from a winter wound in Amalfi, and after demobilisation returned to his previous occupation without grave reluctance. His wife had suffered from the tedium and the huge accumulation of war's minor difficulties more deeply than he, and it was she who proposed, in the first autumn after the fighting stopped, that they should spend a few weeks in the relatively untroubled air, and among the splendid flesh-pots, of non-combatant Ireland.

When the war was over, the victorious but thin-ribbed English discovered that Ireland, for so long a synonym of hunger and discontent, had become something like an Egyptian granary. The victims of old oppression had meat upon their tables and butter in their lordly dishes, while the heirs of the haughty

Ascendancy, of the barons in their Pale and the squires in their parks, fed sadly on offal from the Argentine and the confected fats of chemical industry. So week after week, in their hungry thousands, the famished conquerors were humbly crossing the narrow sea to fill their bellies with neutral beef and mutton that had not – they now were thankful – been sacrificed to any common good.

After three weeks in Kerry, the Latimers were spending a few days in Dublin before returning home, when he, going into their hotel one evening, was halted outside by a girl who held in front of him a wooden collecting-box.

'What's it for?' he asked.

'For the language,' she said.

'What language?'

'The Irish language, of course.'

'I don't understand. Why should

you collect money for a language?'

'So that we can teach it. It's to pay the teachers.'

'And who's going to be taught to speak it?'

'Every one of us. Or so they say.'

'Do you think that's a good thing?'

'I do not!' said the girl. 'I wouldn't speak it myself!'

'Here's half a crown for honesty,' said Latimer, and climbed the steps.

In the lounge he discovered his wife in a group of six or seven people seated round a table on which were twelve or fourteen cocktails, for which two warm and hearty men were disputing the privilege to pay. He was not much surprised. He knew that his wife had arranged to meet an old school-friend and her husband, and he was well aware of her faculty for gathering company, both old friends and new, with a celerity that he could never match. But he was astonished beyond measure when, in the midst of inaccurate but genial introduction, he perceived, with her back to the light, Corinna.

'You know her, don't you?' said his wife. 'She told me that you're old friends. Her husband is Nick's cousin, but he's not here and Nick hasn't come either. So like the Irish, isn't it? Darling, we've all been drinking far too much, you must hurry and catch us up.'

'This is a surprise,' he said.

'You haven't changed a bit,' she answered.

'But you have.'

'My hair,' she said. 'I used to hide behind it. But then I realised what a nuisance it was, and had it cut off.'

'It suits you,' he said, and looked

at her with a sudden greed of attention while the great artery above his heart beat with a perceptible and disconcerting vigour. The soft roundness of her face had become an exquisite tension between cheek-bone and jaw, her eyes seemed the larger in consequence, and her short hair, finely curling, showed the delicate firmness of her head.

'It's incredible,' he said.

'That we should meet again?'

'That Time should be your beauty-parlour.'

'That's Italy!' she said. 'Your wife told me you were in Italy. You've been practising compliments in Rome.'

'On the contrary, I assure you. I was in Trieste with Tito's votaries.'

'Tony spent most of the war with the Northern Patrol and running convoys to Russia. His notion of being romantic is to build a roaring fire, close all the windows, and create a fug that brings the tears to your eyes.'

'Tony's your husband?'

'Yes. I'm an old married woman now. I've got two children.'

'We have three.'

'What a lot can happen in ten years! A war and two families!'

'I've had a very quiet ten years, except for a battle or two.'

'Well, so have I. There wasn't much hectic gaiety in being a wife and mother in the south of England during the war. It's only in the last few weeks that I've got my hands clean.'

'Do you remember driving to the Castle in Edinburgh?'

'Of course.'

'Do make the conversation general!' cried Mrs. Latimer. 'We're all trying not to listen, but my own ears are vibrating furiously, and I'm not the worst. Where have you been, darling?'

'I went to see Michael again.'

'Is he any more cheerful?'

'Someone has asked him to write an article about a very brilliant young Irish dramatist, whose name I can't remember, and he's had to refuse because he isn't quarrelling with him at present. Apparently no Irishman can write about any other Irishman unless they're in a state of open hostility.'

'How very odd. So incense doesn't make the heart grow fonder?'

For half an hour they spoke of the meals they had lately eaten. Food, food and drink, was the English topic in the first years of their victory — the world had rarely seen a hungrier triumph and in their laurelled heads were childish dreams of sugared cakes. They spoke of steaks with reverence, of cheese with sober joy. Ireland, said one of them, was in danger of acquiring a population of new Protestants, as hunger, that once had stripped her, now drew to her green acres her over-taxed and under-nourished neighbours. Ireland of the many famines, now glistening with fat, was England's dream of joy; and the conquerors talked of cream.

Then Corinna said she must go. She had to call for her husband, they were dining with a cousin of his.

'Let me take you,' said Latimer.

'Don't be late,' said his wife. 'We have a table at Jammet's.'

They went out, Corinna cool but he embarrassed.

With shuddering decision a taxi-cab was pulled abruptly to a halt, and the driver leaned towards them. He was an oldish man, burly of frame, with a friendly purple face and a watery eye. Latimer gave him the address and got in. As violently as he had stopped, the driver started again, and a moment later nearly ran a cyclist down.

'He isn't very clever, is he?' said Corinna.

'Does it matter?'

'It may, if he meets someone as stupid as himself. I don't want to die with you.'

'Did your Uncle Henry ever discover that we didn't see the match?'

'No, I don't think so.'

'You didn't tell him?'

'I never told anyone.'

'Nor did I.'

'I've often tried to remember what we talked about. We talked all the time, and I've forgotten everything we said. What did we talk about?'

'Queen Dido and Byzantium.'

'It doesn't seem likely, but tell me more.'

'Dublin is ten years west of Edinburgh. We've less time than we had.'

The driver swerved widely to pass a halted tramcar, and in the lurching cab, filled momentarily with yellow light, Corinna fell into Latimer's arms, and made no move to escape again when his hands closed upon her shoulder and her side. The minutes passed – three, four, or five – before she moved away and said, 'We must be nearly there. Do I look as though you had been kissing me?'

'You look as if God had been kissing you,' he answered a trifle breathlessly.

'I don't think Tony would believe a

story like that,' she said, and took out her powder-box. Then peering through the window, exclaimed, 'But where are we? We haven't come the proper way! I'm sure we haven't!'

She beat upon the sliding glass that divided them from the driver, and when he drew it open, asked him sharply, 'Do you know where we are?'

'I do not!' he said with wild vexation in his husky voice. 'I'm lost entirely.'

'Well!' she said. 'What do we do now?'

The driver, aware that he owed them some explanation, turned his purple face and shouted, 'It's drunk I am! As drunk as a pig!' And angrily closed the sliding glass.

'But this is dangerous,' she said, and let Latimer take her hand.

'He's going very slowly now. We

shan't come to any harm,' he
answered.

Again the driver opened the slide
between them, and now in a more
affable tone declared, 'But it's all
right for you! I'm not charging you
for this.' And pulled down his flag.

'Is that any comfort?' she asked.

'It's the handsomest thing I ever
heard! *Bonosque soles effugere* –.'

'Darling, you're not drunk too?'

'No, of course not. I'm misquoting
Horace. Or is it Martial? I believe
it's Martial.'

'But what does it mean?'

'You learnt Latin at school, didn't
you?'

'What difference does that make?'

'None at all, none at all. But we
haven't time to talk about education,
have we? Listen to what I'm saying,
it's most important. *Solesque* – no,
that's wrong, you've put me off.

Bonosque soles effugere atque abire sentit, qui nobis pereunt et non imputantur. – There now! Aren't we in luck??'

'How do I know, unless you tell me what it means?'

'Just what the driver said. No one's going to charge this to our account. Ireland, God bless it, is neutral still!'

The driver, deciding to try his luck in the opposite direction, turned right-about in the breadth of the street without slackening speed, and threw Corinna on to Latimer's breast before she could decide whether that was her intention or not. He, clasping her and advantage firmly together, began without loss of time to kiss her fondly, repeatedly, and with such enthusiasm as was bound to provoke a reciprocal warmth. The driver, looking this way and that but scorning to ask the help of any passer-by, turned east, west, north, and south to find a familiar landmark and the address that he had long since forgotten.

He looked for it in Ballsbridge and

the neighbourhood of Glasnevin cemetery. He had a notion it might be in Ringsend, and not long after was out past Kilmainham Gaol and on the road to Mullingar. But open country frightened him, and he turned in a great hurry and drove at high speed past Guinness's Brewery, then loitered thoughtfully on College Green, and slowly, like a man in a trance, patrolled O'Connell Street and Grafton Street. He circumnavigated Merrion Square and went twice round St. Stephen's Green to see if it was there. He remembered Rathmines and with fresh hope increased his speed again, but was perplexed by many streets that looked the same, and with a salmon's instinct in the spring turned north again to dawdle by the Liffey. Memory stirred more strongly in him, but a memory quite irrelevant, and for a long time he waited by the gate of the Rotunda Hospital, where he had been born. When at last he returned to Latimer's hotel and deposited Latimer, alone, he was nearly sober.

Latimer paid him off, and turning to go in encountered for the second time the girl with the collecting-box to whom he had spoken earlier in the evening.

She held the box in front of him, a little wearily. 'For the language,' she begged.

'Go home,' he told her, 'for you're wasting your time. There are no words for it in any language. Joy's inenarrable, as every cabman knows!'

SEALSKIN TROUSERS

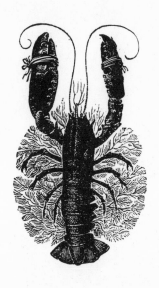

SEALSKIN TROUSERS

I am not mad. It is necessary to realise that, to accept it as a fact about which there can be no dispute. I have been seriously ill for some weeks, but that was the result of shock. A double or conjoint shock: for as well as the obvious concussion of a brutal event, there was the more dreadful necessity of recognising the material evidence of a happening so monstrously implausible that even my friends here, who in general are quite extraordinarily kind and understanding, will not believe in the occurrence, though they cannot deny it or otherwise explain – I mean explain away – the clear and simple testimony of what was left.

I, or course, realised very quickly what had happened, and since then I have more than once remembered that poor Coleridge teased his un-quiet mind, quite unnecessarily in his case, with just such a possibility; or impossibility, as the world would call it. 'If a man could pass through Paradise in a dream,' he wrote, 'and have a flower presented to him as a pledge that his soul had really been there, and if he found that flower in his hand when he woke – Ay, and what then?'

But what if he had dreamt of Hell and wakened with his hand burnt by the fire? Or of Chaos, and seen another face stare at him from the looking-glass? Coleridge does not push the question far. He was too timid. But I accepted the evidence, and while I was ill I thought seriously about the whole proceeding, in detail and in sequence of detail. I thought, indeed, about little else. To begin with, I admit, I was badly shaken, but gradually my mind cleared and my vision improved, and because I was patient and persevering – that needed discipline – I can now say that I know what happened. I have indeed, by a conscious intellectual effort, *seen and heard* what happened. This is how it began....

How very unpleasant! she thought.

She had come down the great natural steps on the sea-cliff to the ledge that narrowly gave access, round the angle of it, to the western face which today was sheltered from the breeze and warmed by the afternoon sun. At the beginning of the week she and her fiancé, Charles Sellin, had found their way to an almost hidden shelf, a deep veranda sixty feet above the white-veined water. It was rather bigger than a billiard-table and nearly as private as an abandoned lighthouse. Twice they had spent some blissful hours there. She had a good head for heights, and Sellin was indifferent to scenery. There had been nothing vulgar, no physical contact, in their bliss together on this oceanic gazebo, for on each occasion she had been reading Héaloin's *Studies in Biology* and he Lenin's *What is to be Done?*

Their relations were already marital, not because their mutual passion could brook no pause, but rather out of fear lest their friends might despise them for chastity and so conjecture some oddity or impotence in their nature. Their behaviour, however, was very decently circumspect, and they already conducted themselves, in public and out of doors, as if they had been married for several years. They did not regard the seclusion of the cliffs as an opportunity for secret embracing, but were content that the sun should warm and colour their skin; and let their anxious minds be soothed by the surge and cavernous colloquies of the sea. Now, while Charles was writing letters in the little fishing-hotel a mile away, she had come back to their sandstone ledge, and Charles would join her in an hour or two. She was still reading *Studies in Biology*.

But their gazebo, she perceived, was already occupied, and occupied by a person of the most embarrassing appearance. He was quite unlike Charles. He was not only naked, but obviously robust, brown-hued, and extremely hairy. He sat on the very edge of the rock, dangling his legs over the sea, and down his spine ran a ridge of hair like the dark stripe on a donkey's back, and on his shoulder-blades grew patches of hair like the wings of a bird. Unable in her disappointment to be sensible and leave at once, she lingered for a moment and saw to her relief that he was not quite naked. He wore trousers of a dark brown colour, very low at the waist, but sufficient to cover his haunches. Even so, even with that protection for her modesty, she could not stay and read biology in his company.

To show her annoyance, and let him become aware of it, she made a little impatient sound; and turning to go, looked back to see if he had heard.

He swung himself round and glared at her, more angry on the instant than she had been. He had thick eyebrows, large dark eyes, a broad snub nose, a big mouth. 'You're Roger Fairfield!' she exclaimed in surprise.

He stood up and looked at her intently. 'How do you know?' he asked.

'Because I remember you,' she answered, but then felt a little confused, for what she principally remembered was the brief notoriety he had acquired, in his final year at Edinburgh University, by swimming on a rough autumn day from North Berwick to the Bass Rock to win a bet of five pounds.

The story had gone briskly round

the town for a week, and everybody knew that he and some friends had been lunching, too well for caution, before the bet was made. His friends, however, grew quickly sober when he took to the water, and in a great fright informed the police, who called out the lifeboat. But they searched in vain, for the sea was running high, until in calm water under the shelter of the Bass they saw his head, dark on the water, and pulled him aboard. He seemed none the worse for his adventure, but the police charged him with disorderly behaviour and he was fined two pounds for swimming without a regulation costume.

'We met twice,' she said, 'once at a dance and once in Mackie's when we had coffee together. About a year ago. There were several of us there, and we knew the man you came in with. I remember you perfectly.'

He stared harder, his eyes narrowing, a vertical wrinkle dividing his forehead. 'I'm a little short-sighted too,' she said with a nervous laugh.

'My sight's very good,' he answered, 'but I find it difficult to recognise people. Human beings are so much alike.'

'That's one of the rudest remarks I've ever heard!'

'Surely not?'

'Well, one does like to be remembered. It isn't pleasant to be told that one's a nonentity.'

He made an impatient gesture. 'That isn't what I meant, and I do recognise you now. I remember your voice. You have a distinctive voice and a pleasant one. F sharp in the octave below middle C is your note.'

'Is that the only way in which you can distinguish people?'

'It's as good as any other.'

'But you don't remember my name?'

'No,' he said.

'I'm Elizabeth Barford.'

He bowed and said, 'Well, it was a dull party, wasn't it? The occasion, I mean, when we drank coffee together.'

'I don't agree with you. I thought it was very amusing, and we all enjoyed ourselves. Do you remember Charles Sellin?'

'No.'

'Oh, you're hopeless,' she exclaimed. 'What is the good of meeting people if you're going to forget all about them?'

'I don't know,' he said. 'Let us sit down, and you can tell me.'

He sat again on the edge of the

rock, his legs dangling, and looking over his shoulder at her, said, 'Tell me: what is the good of meeting people?'

She hesitated, and answered, 'I like to make friends. That's quite natural, isn't it? – But I came here to read.'

'Do you read standing?'

'Of course not,' she said, and smoothing her skirt tidily over her knees, sat down beside him. 'What a wonderful place this is for a holiday. Have you been here before?'

'Yes, I know it well.'

'Charles and I came a week ago. Charles Sellin, I mean, whom you don't remember. We're going to be married, you know. In about a year, we hope.'

'Why did you come here?'

'We wanted to be quiet, and in these islands one is fairly secure against interruption. We're both working quite hard.'

'Working!' he mocked. 'Don't waste time, waste your life instead.'

'Most of us have to work, whether we like it or not.'

He took the book from her lap, and opening it read idly a few lines, turned a dozen pages and read with a yawn another paragraph.

'Your friends in Edinburgh,' she said, 'were better-off than ours. Charles and I, and all the people we know, have got to make our living.'

'Why?' he asked.

'Because if we don't we shall starve,' she snapped.

'And if you avoid starvation – what then?'

'It's possible to hope,' she said stiffly, 'that we shall be of some use in the world.'

'Do you agree with this?' he asked,

smothering a second yawn, and read from the book: '*The physical factor in a germ-cell is beyond our analysis or assessment, but can we deny subjectivity to the primordial initiatives? It is easier, perhaps, to assume that mind comes late in development, but the assumption must not be established on the grounds that we can certainly deny self-expression to the cell. It is common knowledge that the mind may influence the body both greatly and in little unseen ways; but how it is done, we do not know. Psychobiology is still in its infancy.*'

'It's fascinating, isn't it?' she said.

'How do you propose,' he asked, 'to be of use to the world?'

'Well, the world needs people who have been educated – educated to think – and one does hope to have a little influence in some way.'

'Is a little influence going to make any difference? Don't you think that what the world needs is to develop a new sort of mind? It needs a new primordial directive, or quite a lot of them, perhaps. But psychobiology is still in its infancy, and you don't know how such changes come about, do you? And you can't foresee when you *will* know, can you?'

'No, of course not. But science is advancing so quickly –.'

'In fifty thousand years?' he interrupted. 'Do you think you will know by then?'

'It's difficult to say,' she answered seriously, and was gathering her thoughts for a careful reply when again he interrupted, rudely, she thought, and quite irrelevantly. His attention had strayed from her and her book to the sea beneath, and he was looking down as though searching for something. 'Do you swim?' he asked.

'Rather well,' she said.

'I went in just before high water, when the weed down there was all brushed in the opposite direction. You never get bored by the sea, do you?'

'I've never seen enough of it,' she said. 'I want to live on an island, a little island, and hear it all round me.'

'That's very sensible of you,' he answered with more warmth in his voice. 'That's uncommonly sensible for a girl like you.'

'What sort of a girl do you think I am?' she demanded, vexation in her accent, but he ignored her and pointed his brown arm to the horizon: 'The colour has thickened within the last few minutes. The sea was quite pale on the skyline, and now it's a belt of indigo. And the writing has changed. The lines of foam on the water, I mean. Look at that! There's a submerged rock out there, and always, about half an hour after the ebb has started to run, but more clearly when there's an off-shore wind, you can see those two

little whirlpools and the circle of white round them. You see the figure they make? It's like this, isn't it?'

With a splinter of stone he drew a diagram on the rock.

'Do you know what it is?' he asked. 'It's the figure the Chinese call the T'ai Chi. They say it represents the origin of all created things. And it's the sign manual of the sea.'

'But those lines of foam must run into every conceivable shape,' she protested.

'Oh, they do. They do indeed. But it isn't often you can read them. – There he is!' he exclaimed, leaning forward and staring into the water sixty feet below. 'That's him, the old villain!'

From his sitting position, pressing hard down with his hands and thrusting against the face of the rock with his heels, he hurled himself into space, and straightening in mid-air broke the smooth green surface of the water with no more splash than a harpoon would have made. A solitary razorbill, sunning himself on a shelf below, fled hurriedly out to sea, and half a dozen white birds, startled by the sudden movement, rose in the air crying 'Kittiwake! Kittiwake!'

Elizabeth screamed loudly, scrambled to her feet with clumsy speed, then knelt again on the edge of the rock and peered down. In the slowly heaving clear water she could see a pale shape moving, now striped by the dark weed that grew in tangles under the flat foot of the rock, now lost in the shadowy deepness where the tangles were rooted. In a minute or two his head rose from the sea, he shook bright drops from his hair, and looked up at her, laughing. Firmly grasped in his right hand, while he trod water, he held up an enormous blue-black lobster for her admiration. Then he threw it on to the flat rock beside him, and swiftly climbing out of the sea, caught it again and held it, cautious of its bite, till he found a piece of string in his trouser-pocket. He shouted to her,

'I'll tie its claws, and you can take it home for your supper!'

She had not thought it possible to climb the sheer face of the cliff, but from its forefoot he mounted by steps and handholds invisible from above, and pitching the tied lobster on to the floor of the gazebo, came nimbly over the edge.

'That's a bigger one than you've ever seen in your life before,' he boasted. 'He weighs fourteen pounds, I'm certain of it. Fourteen pounds at least. Look at the size of his right claw! He could crack a coconut with that. He tried to crack my ankle when I was swimming an hour ago, and got into his hole before I could catch him. But I've caught him now, the brute. He's had more than twenty years of crime, that black boy. He's twenty-four or twenty-five by the look of him. He's older than you, do you realise that? Unless you're a lot older than you look. How old are you?'

But Elizabeth took no interest in the lobster. She had retreated until she stood with her back to the rock, pressed hard against it, the palms of her hands fumbling on the stone as if feeling for a secret lock or bolt that might give her entrance into it. Her face was white, her lips pale and tremulous.

He looked round at her, when she made no answer, and asked what the matter was.

Her voice was faint and frightened. 'Who are you?' she whispered, and the whisper broke into a stammer. 'What are you?'

His expression changed and his face, with the waterdrops on it, grew hard as a rock shining undersea. 'It's only a few minutes,' he said, 'since you appeared to know me quite well. You addressed me as Roger Fairfield, didn't you?'

'But a name's not everything. It doesn't tell you enough.'

'What more do you want to know?'

Her voice was so strained and thin that her words were like the shadow of words, or words shivering in the cold: 'To jump like that, into the sea – it wasn't human!'

The coldness of his face wrinkled to a frown. 'That's a curious remark to make.'

'You would have killed yourself if – if —.'

He took a seaward step again, looked down at the calm green depths below, and said, 'You're exaggerating, aren't you? It's not much more than fifty feet, sixty perhaps, and the water's deep. –

179

Here, come back! Why are you running away?'

'Let me go!' she cried. 'I don't want to stay here. I – I'm frightened.'

'That's unfortunate. I hadn't expected this to happen.'

'Please let me go!'

'I don't think I shall. Not until you've told me what you're frightened of.'

'Why,' she stammered, 'why do you wear fur trousers?'

He laughed, and still laughing caught her round the waist and pulled her towards the edge of the rock. 'Don't be alarmed,' he said. 'I'm not going to throw you over. But if you insist on a conversation about trousers, I think we should sit down again. Look at the smoothness of the water, and its colour, and the light in the depths of it: have you ever seen anything lovelier? Look at the sky: that's calm enough, isn't it? Look at that fulmar sailing past: he's not worrying, so why should you?'

She leaned away from him, all her weight against the hand that held her waist, but his arm was strong and he seemed unaware of any strain on it. Nor did he pay attention to the distress she was in – she was sobbing dryly, like a child who has cried too long – but continued talking in a light and pleasant conversational tone until the muscles of her body tired and relaxed, and she sat within his enclosing arm, making no more effort to escape, but timorously conscious of his hand upon her side so close beneath her breast.

'I needn't tell you,' he said, 'the conventional reasons for wearing trousers. There are people, I know, who sneer at all conventions, and some conventions deserve their sneering. But not the trouser-convention. No, indeed! So we can admit the necessity of the garment, and pass to consideration of the material. Well, I like sitting on rocks, for one thing, and for such a hobby this is the best stuff in the world. It's very durable, yet soft and comfortble. I can slip into the sea for half an hour without doing it any harm, and when I come out to sun myself on the rock again, it doesn't feel cold and clammy. Nor does it fade in the sun or shrink with the wet. Oh, there are plenty of reasons for having one's trousers made of stuff like this.'

'And there's a reason,' she said, 'that you haven't told me.'

'Are you quite sure of that?'

She was calmer now, and her breathing was controlled.

But her face was still white, and her lips were softly nervous when she asked him, 'Are you going to kill me?'

'Kill you? Good heavens, no! Why should I do that?'

'For fear of my telling other people.'

'And what precisely would you tell them?'

'You know.'

'You jump to conclusions far too quickly: that's your trouble. Well, it's a pity for your sake, and a nuisance for me. I don't think I can let you take that lobster home for your supper after all. I don't, in fact, think you will go home for your supper.'

Her eyes grew dark again with fear, her mouth opened, but before she could speak he pulled her to him and closed it, not asking leave, with a roughly occludent kiss.

'That was to prevent you from screaming. I hate to hear people scream,' he told her, smiling as he spoke. 'But this' – he kissed her again, now gently and in a more protracted embrace – 'that was because I wanted to.'

'You mustn't!' she cried.

'But I have,' he said.

'I don't understand myself! I can't understand what has happened —.'

'Very little yet,' he murmured.

'Something terrible has happened!'

'A kiss? Am I so repulsive?'

'I don't mean that. I mean something inside me. I'm not – at least I think I'm not – I'm not frightened now!'

'You have no reason to be.'

'I have every reason in the world.

But I'm not! I'm not frightened –
but I want to cry.'

'Then cry,' he said soothingly, and
made her pillow her cheek against his
breast. 'But you can't cry comfort-
ably with that ridiculous contraption
on your nose.'

He took from her the horn-
rimmed spectacles she wore, and
threw them into the sea.

'Oh!' she exclaimed. 'My glasses!
– Oh, why did you do that? Now I
can't see. I can't see at all without my
glasses!'

'It's all right,' he assured her. 'You
really won't need them. The
refraction,' he added vaguely, 'will be
quite different.'

As if this small but unexpected act
of violence had brought to the
boiling-point her desire for tears,
they bubbled over, and because she
threw her arms about him in a sort of

fond despair, and snuggled close, sobbing vigorously still, he felt the warm drops trickle down his skin, and from his skin she drew into her eyes the saltness of the sea, which made her weep the more. He stroked her hair with a strong but soothing hand, and when she grew calm and lay still in his arms, her emotion spent, he sang quietly to a little enchanting tune a song that began:

'I am a Man upon the land,
I am a Selkie in the sea,
And when I'm far from every strand
My home it is on Sule Skerry.'

After the first verse or two she freed herself from his embrace, and sitting up listened gravely to the song. Then she asked him, 'Shall I ever understand?'

'It's not a unique occurrence,' he told her. 'It has happened quite often

186

before, as I suppose you know. In Cornwall and Brittany and among the Western Isles of Scotland; that's where people have always been interested in seals, and understood them a little, and where seals from time to time have taken human shape. The one thing that's unique in our case, in my metamorphosis, is that I am the only seal-man who has ever become a Master of Arts of Edinburgh University. Or, I believe, of any university. I am the unique and solitary example of a sophisticated seal-man.'

'I must look a perfect fright,' she said. 'It was silly of me to cry. Are my eyes very red?'

'The lids are a little pink – not unattractively so – but your eyes are as dark and lovely as a mountain pool in October, on a sunny day in October. They're much improved since I threw your spectacles away.'

'I needed them, you know. I feel quite stupid without them. But tell me why you came to the University – and how? How could you do it?'

'My dear girl – what is your name, by the way? I've quite forgotten.'

'Elizabeth!' she said angrily.

'I'm so glad, it's my favourite human name. – But you don't really want to listen to a lecture on psychobiology?'

'I want to know *how*. You must tell me!'

'Well, you remember, don't you, what your book says about the primordial initiatives? But it needs a footnote there to explain that they're not exhausted till quite late in life. The germ-cells, as you know, are always renewing themselves, and they keep their initiatives though they nearly always follow the chosen pattern except in the case of certain illnesses, or under special direction. The direction of the mind, that is. And the glands have got a lot to do in a full metamorphosis, the renal first and then the pituitary, as you would expect. It isn't approved of – making the change, I mean – but every now and then one of us does it, just for a frolic in the general way, but in my case there was a special reason.'

'Tell me,' she said again.

'It's too long a story.'

'I want to know.'

'There's been a good deal of unrest, you see, among my people in the last few years: doubt, and dissatisfaction with our leaders, and scepticism about traditional beliefs – all that sort of thing. We've had a lot of discussion under the surface of the sea about the nature of man, for instance. We had always been taught to believe certain things about him, and recent events didn't seem to bear out what our teachers told us. Some of our younger people got dissatisfied, so I volunteered to go ashore and investigate. I'm still considering the report I shall have to make, and that's why I'm living, at present, a double life. I come ashore to think, and go back to the sea to rest.'

'And what do you think of us?' she asked.

'You're interesting. Very interesting indeed. There are going to be some curious mutations among you before long. Within three or four thousand years, perhaps.'

He stooped and rubbed a little smear of blood from his shin. 'I scratched it on a limpet,' he said. 'The limpets, you know, are the same

190

today as they were four hundred thousand years ago. But human beings aren't nearly so stable.'

'Is that your main impression, that humanity's unstable?'

'That's part of it. But from our point of view there's something much more upsetting. Our people, you see, are quite simple creatures, and because we have relatively few beliefs, we're very much attached to them. Our life is a life of sensation – not entirely, but largely – and we ought to be extremely happy. We were, so long as we were satisfied with sensation and a short undisputed creed. We have some advantages over human beings, you know. Human beings have to carry their own weight about, and they don't know how blissful it is to be unconscious of weight: to be wave-borne, to float on the idle sea, to leap without effort in a curving wave, and look up at the dazzle of the sky through a smother of white water, or dive so easily to the calmness far below and take a haddock from the weed-beds in a sudden rush of appetite. – Talking of haddocks,' he said, 'it's getting late. It's nearly time for fish. And I must give you some instruction before we go. The preliminary phase takes a little while, about five minutes for you, I should think, and then you'll be another creature.'

She gasped, as though already she felt the water's chill, and whispered. 'Not yet! Not yet, please.'

He took her in his arms, and expertly, with a strong caressing hand, stroked her hair, stroked the roundness of her head and the back of her neck and her shoulders, feeling her muscles moving to his touch, and down the hollow of her back to her waist and hips. The head again, neck, shoulders, and spine. Again and again. Strongly and firmly his hand gave her calmness, and presently she whispered, 'You're sending me to sleep.'

'My God!' he exclaimed, 'you mustn't do that! Stand up, stand up, Elizabeth!'

'Yes,' she said, obeying him. 'Yes, Roger. Why did you call yourself Roger? Roger Fairfield?'

'I found the name in a drowned sailor's pay-book. What does that matter now? Look at me, Elizabeth!'

She looked at him, and smiled.

His voice changed, and he said happily, 'You'll be the prettiest seal between Shetland and the Scillies. Now listen. Listen carefully.'

He held her lightly and whispered in her ear. Then kissed her on the lips and cheek, and bending her head back, on the throat. He looked, and saw the colour come deeply into her face.

'Good,' he said. 'That's the first stage. The adrenalin's flowing nicely now. You know about the pituitary, don't you? That makes it easy then. There are two parts in the pituitary gland, the anterior and posterior lobes, and both must act together. It's not difficult, and I'll tell you how.'

Then he whispered again, most urgently, and watched her closely. In a little while he said, 'And now you can take it easy. Let's sit down and wait till you're ready. The actual change won't come till we go down.'

'But it's working,' she said, quietly and happily. 'I can feel it working.'

'Of course it is.'

She laughed triumphantly, and took his hand.

'We've got nearly five minutes to wait,' he said.

'What will it be like? What shall I feel, Roger?'

'The water moving against your side, the sea caressing you and holding you.'

'Shall I be sorry for what I've left behind?'

'No, I don't think so.'

'You didn't like us, then? Tell me what your discovered in the world.'

'Quite simply,' he said, 'that we had been deceived.'

'But I don't know what your belief had been.'

'Haven't I told you? – Well, we in our innocence respected you because you could work, and were willing to work. That seemed to us truly heroic. We don't work at all, you see, and you'll be much happier when you come to us. We who live in the sea don't struggle to keep our heads above water.'

'All my friends worked hard,' she said. 'I never knew anyone who was idle. We had to work, and most of us worked for a good purpose; or so we thought. But you didn't think so?'

'Our teachers had told us,' he said, 'that men endured the burden of human toil to create a surplus of wealth that would give them leisure from the daily task of bread-winning. And in their hard-won leisure, our teachers said, men cultivated wisdom and charity and the fine arts; and became aware of God. – But that's not a true description of the world, is it?'

'No,' she said, 'that's not the truth.'

'No,' he repeated, 'our teachers

were wrong, and we've been deceived.'

'Men are always being deceived, but they get accustomed to learning the facts too late. They grow accustomed to deceit itself.'

'You are braver than we, perhaps. My people will not like to be told the truth.'

'I shall be with you,' she said, and took his hand. But still he stared gloomily at the moving sea.

The minutes passed, and presently she stood up and with quick fingers put off her clothes. 'It's time,' she said.

He looked at her, and his gloom vanished like the shadow of a cloud that the wind has hurried on, and exultation followed like sunlight spilling from the burning edge of a cloud. 'I wanted to punish them,' he cried, 'for robbing me of my faith, and now, by God, I'm punishing them hard. I'm robbing their treasury now, the inner vault of all their treasury! – I hadn't guessed you were so beautiful! The waves when you swim will catch a burnish from you, the sand will shine like silver when you lie down to sleep, and if you can teach the red sea-ware to blush so well, I shan't miss the roses of your world.'

'Hurry,' she said.

He, laughing softly, loosened the leather thong that tied his trousers, stepped out of them, and lifted her in his arms. 'Are you ready?' he asked.

She put her arms round his neck and softly kissed his cheek. Then with a great shout he leapt from the rock, from the little veranda, into the green silk calm of the water far below....

I heard the splash of their descent – I am quite sure I heard the splash – as I came round the corner of the cliff, by the ledge that leads to the little rock veranda, our gazebo, as we called it, but the first thing I noticed, that really attracted my attention, was an enormous blue-black lobster, its huge claws tied with string, that was moving in a rather ludicrous fashion towards the edge. I think it fell over just before I left, but I wouldn't swear to that. Then I saw her book, the *Studies in Biology*, and her clothes.

Her white linen frock with the brown collar and the brown belt, some other garments, and her shoes were all there. And beside them, lying across her shoes, was a pair of sealskin trousers.

I realised immediately, or almost immediately, what had happened.

Or so it seems to me now. And if, as I firmly believe, my apprehension was instantaneous, the faculty of intuition is clearly more important than I had previously supposed. I have, of course, as I said before, given the matter a great deal of thought during my recent illness, but the impression remains that I understood what had happened in a flash, to use a common but illuminating phrase. And no one, need I say? has been able to refute my intuition. No one, that is, has found an alternative explanation for the presence, beside Elizabeth's linen frock, of a pair of sealskin trousers.

I remember also my physical distress at the discovery. My breath, for several minutes I think, came into and went out of my lungs like the hot wind of a dust-storm in the desert. It parched my mouth and grated in my throat. It was, I recall, quite a torment to breathe. But I had to, of course.

Nor did I lose control of myself in spite of the agony, both mental and physical, that I was suffering. I didn't lose control till they began to mock me. Yes, they did, I assure you of that. I heard his voice quite clearly, and honesty compels me to admit that it was singularly sweet and the tune was the most haunting I have ever heard. They were about forty yards away, two seals swimming together, and the evening light was so clear and taut that his voice might have been the vibration of an invisible bow across its coloured bands. He was singing the song that Elizabeth and I had discovered in an album of Scottish music in the little fishing-hotel where we had been living:

'I am a Man upon the land,
I am a Selkie in the sea,
And when I'm far from any strand
I am at home on Sule Skerry!'

But his purpose, you see, was mockery. They were happy, together in the vast simplicity of the ocean, and I, abandoned to the terror of life alone, life among human beings, was lost and full of panic. It was then I began to scream. I could hear myself screaming, it was quite horrible. But I couldn't stop. I had to go on screaming....

The aim of Masterworks Large Print Books is to make reading a more rewarding experience for partially sighted people.

A good range of recreational reading is available in large print, but there remains a shortage of fine literature, and it is the intention of Masterworks to make good this deficiency, by publishing large print editions of erudite titles. Wherever practible, works by winners of the Nobel Prize for Literature will be chosen, together with titles by other distinguished writers.

Type sizes and faces have been carefully researched, and the contrast between the black type and the cream tint of the lightweight paper has been calculated to cause a minimum of strain to the eyes.

All the texts have been completely reset, because of the importance of good type design in books catering for partially sighted readers. The results of research suggest that four different factors are critical in the typography of large print books: the size of the type, its boldness, the way it is spaced, and the use of a consistent typeface. A proper combination of the best typographic features results in a vast improvement in readability.

We would like as many people as possible to be aware of these innovations in large print and hope that readers will recommend the results to others. We welcome suggestions from readers for new titles.

Other titles in this series:

William Golding
THE HOT GATES

A dazzling collection of writings by the Nobel Prize-winning novelist on subjects ranging from Thermopylae to the English Channel, and from **Coral Island** to Jules Verne.

'A book of occasional essays which afford us many fascinating insights into Golding the man. I found the tone of the book singularly attractive. It is highly individual yet profoundly modest; it has an unusual, slightly angular candour, full of painful knowledge and a beautiful humanity; it couldn't be pretentious if it tried . . . even the slightest piece bears the mark of his rare, austere mind and remarkable imagination . . .'
New Society.

1 85290 016 4   *c200pp*

Heinrich Böll

THE LOST HONOUR OF KATHARINA BLUM

Pretty, bright young Katharina Blum falls in love with a young radical lawbreaker on the run from the police. Portrayed by the local press as a whore, a communist sympathizer and an atheist, she becomes the target of anonymous phone calls and threats. Her life ruined and her character and honour trampled by the distortions of a corrupt press she shoots the offending journalist.

This novel is a masterful comment on the law and the press, the labyrinth of social truth, and the relentless collision of fact and fiction.

1 85290 017 2   c200pp

Margaret Yourcenar

ORIENTAL TALES

Translated from the French by Alberto Manguel
in collaboration with the author.

From China to Greece, from the Balkans to
Japan, these tales take us from a portrait of the
painter Wang-Fo, 'who loves the image of
things and not the things themselves' and
whose own work saves him from execution, to
legends of a hero betrayed and then rescued by
love, and to the Indian goddess Kali, who in
her unhappiness discovers 'the emptiness of
desire'. Violence, murder and betrayal all
feature in these stories of love and adventure.

Bernard Levin
THE WAY WE LIVE NOW

Collected in **The Way We Live Now**, from Levin's weekly column in **The Times**, we find arguments for democracy, the rights of theatre critics, the genius of Venice, Isaac Stern and Frank Lloyd Wright. There is condemnation for Mao, Kim Il Sung, writers' conferences and euthanasia.